THE HARL...

b...

NIKKI DEE

Being book two of the Sansome Springs Saga
First Edition 2017

Second Edition

Copyright © 2019 Nikki Dee

ISBN: 9781541069732

ALL RIGHTS RESERVED

ACKNOWLEDGEMENTS

I give thanks to Berrows Worcester Journal, the world's oldest newspaper. Their archive is a joy and an inspiration.

Nikki Dee

The Harlot's Garden
The Harlot's Pride
The Harlot's Horde
Losing Hope
An Ordinary Girl

www.nikkidee.net

CHAPTER ONE

Ruby Morgan wiped a trickle of sweat from her brow and sighed in irritation.

She'd arrived here in the cool of the early morning, wanting to commandeer the single ornate bench that had been installed to mark the opening of the new bridge, and there'd been barely a soul about. She'd shivered deliciously in the crisp breeze that whipped along the Severn.

Now though, the sun was high in the sky and a multitude had gathered around her until she was stifled by the sticky press of bodies that prevented a breath of air from reaching her. She'd retained possession of the bench, but it had been a battle.

The sun burned down on her head, her eyes were sore but above all that her bladder screamed for relief and she doubted she could hold on. *Where the bloody hell was Bella?*

She scanned the laughing crowd again and almost wept as she saw her friend cheerfully elbowing her way past a crowd of men, pausing to take a sip of ale from one and pinch the cheek of another.

'Sorry I'm late Rube it was...'

'Not now.' Ruby relinquished responsibility for protecting their vantage point and ran for the bushes, lifting her skirts as she went. The cat calls that followed in her wake did nothing to deter her. She had to go.

The blessed relief was such that she practically skipped back to the bench, pausing only to execute a curtsy to her audience. Bella grinned in appreciation and added her own applause.

'I'd given you up for lost, what kept you?'

'Every bloody pathway is packed, and the daft sods have even closed off the track behind the Hop Pole. I got half way and had to double back. They didn't want to let me on the bridge, they say it's too crowded and in danger of collapsing, but that was only Martha Ridgeley's husband and I've always had a way with him.' She winked and licked her lips.

'I hope Mary can get through. There was barely a soul on here when she left me.'

'With her temper I don't think there's any doubt about that.'

They sat quietly for a time watching as their neighbours, more used to the treadmill of back breaking work and insufficient food, paraded about wearing their church best and relishing the chance to kick up their heels and have some fun.

They smiled at the nervous young men who eyed up giggling girls who pretended not to notice, despite their scarlet cheeks. Those same young men tossed challenges to one another, any excuse to demonstrate their bravery or virility.

Raucous bursts of song broke out and jokes and teasing ebbed and flowed easily. The air thickened with the heat of bodies and fumes from the flagons of drink that flew along, passed from hand to hand.

Ruby took a mouthful and grinned as she passed it on to Bella, happier now she had she had her friend by her side.

'Have you heard from your Ellie, any word on what ails her?' Bella asked.

Ruby shook her head. 'You know what they say. Marry in haste…'

She and her twin had an uneasy relationship at the best of times. They'd been inseparable until the age of fourteen when they'd been sent in different directions, not meeting again for seven years, by which time they were young women with differences that seemed irreconcilable. Their love was still there, and they were overjoyed to be re-united, but life had treated them in disparate ways and finding common ground had been a struggle. Both had needed to make allowances and learn when to keep their mouths shut.

Ellie had recently married a respectable widower. She respected him and loved his sons. He owned a fine home and was comfortably off and, as all she'd ever wanted was a home and a family, she accepted his proposal.

'She's lost weight and looks as miserable as sin when she thinks no-ones looking, though she swears there's nothing wrong.'

Bella clicked her fingers. 'He's a few years younger than her, could that be a problem? I mean for me it'd be a bonus but…' She winked.

Ruby laughed. 'Promise not to change Bel.'

'Not me. But what's to be done about Ellie?'

'If I don't see her in the next few days I'll have to call on them and I don't think her fancy new husband is going to like that very much at all. She told me a while back that he doesn't want the likes of me around his boys. But If she needs me, he'll have to deal with it.'

Giving out this much information was quite a departure, she rarely said much when it came to family business and Bella clapped her mouth shut. She loved Ruby dearly but had neither time nor patience for her stuck-up twin, if Ellie was having a tough time in her marriage, then Bella would savour the details.

'I've kept my ears to the ground and he's not the man she thinks he is, of that I'm certain.'

Bella nodded. 'I've certainly heard some pretty ripe talk about him.'

Ruby raised her chin defiantly and grinned at her friend. 'Don't you fret, I'll sort him out in good time and I certainly won't let him cast a cloud over our day.'

'Don't you want to know what I've heard about him though Rube?'

Ruby took a gulp of red wine and wiped her hand across her mouth. 'If you asked anyone here if they'd heard anything bad about me, what do you reckon they'd say?'

'Well, I don't know wh...'

'I've no time for the kind of dirt that's been looked for. I want to know what he's done to my sister and I'll only get that from her. Now let's forget about the bloody Pargeters and enjoy ourselves. You made me take this day off, it's up to you to see I enjoy it. Enough of all that other nonsense.'

The delicious whisper of gossip wafted out of reach.

...at Worcester, the company was genteel and numerous and the various places of amusement were extremely well attended. However, a pretty strong detachment of the light fingered tribe attended on the occasion and, we fear, reaped a plentiful harvest. One gentleman was hustled by two or three of the fraternity and lost a pocket book containing bankers notes
(Copyright and courtesy of the Worcester News)

CHAPTER TWO

Ruby's life was structured around the needs of Sansome Springs, the pleasure gardens that she'd built on the outskirts of the city. August was without question her busiest month and a scorcher like today would have attracted throngs, she was regretting caving in to Mary and Bella and closing for the day.

The gardens occupied land given to Ruby by Ma Jebb, the bawdy house owner, and thief protector, who'd saved her life. Ma had been given the land by the only man she'd ever cared for and Ruby had named her gardens after him in honour of them both.

From the moment she'd first walked on the cool, sweet grass to collect water from the spring she'd cherished the sense of peace that she felt. She wanted others to enjoy the clean beauty of her spring, not fear the wilderness that surrounded it.

Determination and hard slog, combined with a terrifying amount of money, enabled her to to pull off a miracle. She'd transformed the overgrown and heavily wooded terrain into an elegant parkland laid out around a natural spring. She'd had channels dug out to allow streams of cool water to wend their way, almost naturally, alongside pathways and around groups of seats. There were fountains and waterfalls to cool the air and a carefully planted selection of trees and shrubs complemented the wild roses, lavender and rosemary that mother nature had long since established.

Small raised platforms were scattered, apparently randomly, within the planted areas. A visitor could stroll in the perfumed air and choose whether to watch a comedy sketch being played out, listen to a poetry recital, or marvel as an acrobat practised his routine.

News of the gambling salon at the far edge of the gardens spread far and wide and regularly attracted men from miles around. It was a comfortable and stylish club with mature staff and a strictly regulated admittance policy. A ticket to the gardens didn't guarantee entrance to the gaming rooms. The dress and manners required were of the highest standard and she'd discovered that refusing entry to the foolish and wild young men who periodically tried their luck simply added to its desirability.

A dining hall served hot meals for diners and would also provide picnic baskets for families who preferred to sit outside.

At the other end of the gardens, as far away from the casino, lay a grassy common land where families could laze a day away watching bowling or archery competitions.

Being situated on slightly higher ground than the city itself, the gardens benefitted from fresh breezes that those down below lacked. The hovels that clustered at the river's edge were unseen from this point and there was just enough distance to allow the Severn to present herself as a shining ribbon of silver beauty.

Ruby's pleasure gardens had become the pride of the Midlands. They were perfectly placed on a broad swathe of land sandwiched between the Worcester - Birmingham canal, and the Severn, meaning visitors came from much further afield than Worcester.

Building and promoting this attraction had dominated Ruby's life for years, into these gardens she happily devoted all her passion and love, her energy and creativity. Everything she was unable to bestow on the people that surrounded her.

Her proud boast was that they never closed and that was a claim she was loath to relinquish. It had taken weeks of argument and persuasion by Mary and Bella to convince her that this was one day that she couldn't ignore.

Once she had made that decision however she was determined to squeeze every bit of goodness out of the event. A day away from the love of her life would be a waste were it not filled with fun and excitement.

...pains have been taken in the formation of walks, erecting seats about the hills, that we are not surprised at the preference which has been recently so decidedly given a place on which nature has lavished her beauties with an unsparing hand and has presented her admirers with abundant sources of contemplation and delight. (Copyright and courtesy of the Worcester News)

CHAPTER THREE

Ruby's doubts faded as the crowd continued to grow. The bridge was so overloaded the marshals officiously ordered those near either end off. They all congregated below, lining the river on both sides. Closing for the day had been the right choice. Had she been her usual pig-headed self she'd be stuck out there on her own, missing out on this excitement.

The people on the river banks set up their own parties and the extra room on the bridge meant there was space for a bit of pushing and shoving, good natured way of letting of a bit of energy. It had been a long day, but the celebratory and generous mood lingered.

At a time of national hardship, what with the shortage of cheap grain, little paid work and none to look forward to, the excuse to forget the misery of day-to-day struggle and dive wholeheartedly into a celebration such as this was widely embraced.

Ruby drank from a bottle that was pushed into her hand and then passed it on, smiling as she caught sight of Mary bearing a basket of food for them.

'Sight for sore eyes you are girl.' Bella's hands dived under the covering cloth before Mary could twist it out of her reach.

'Greedy cow, wait a minute, can't you?'

'I can now.' Bella said through a spray of crumbs. 'I'm bleeding starving though. I've been here for hours.'

Ruby took the basket from Mary and gave her a seat before turning to Bella. 'You haven't been here as long as me, so I get first pick, you sit and wait.'

She turned back to Mary. 'She was late, messing about with some fellow.'

'Oh Bella!'

'He wouldn't have let me through without.'

'Well I managed!'

'Ay well, your sour face won't attract them like my pretty face does. It's not easy, being me.' Bella smirked.

'Pretty face my eye. Tits hanging out for all the world to see is what draws them to you.'

Bella poked out her tongue and snatched another pie.

They ate and drank and teased in perfect harmony. They'd endured hardships and been there for each other for so long that their trust and understanding was unshakeable.

'Oh, that's better, my belly thought my throat had been cut. Bless you Mary.' Ruby said, rubbing her belly in satisfaction. 'Let's tuck this basket away and have a bit of fun now it's cooler. We won't have much longer to wait.'

From their position in the centre of the bridge they could look left see the approach from St Johns and to their right, the route into the city. And the entirety choked with people, singing, dancing and trying to push each other into the river.

Ruby laughed out loud when strong male hands grasp her around the waist and drew her into a dance and being passed along a line from hand to hand and then back to the start.

This feeling of belonging was a novelty, she'd grown accustomed to being shunned having been born dirt poor but then receiving an education made her awkward, an oddity.

She'd endured hard times and taken paths others might have shunned but she'd never lied about what she did or apologised for it. She clung to her dignity and had always paid her way, taking nothing that wasn't her due. She was comfortable with her place in the world and thankful that the friends who'd stood by her when she was at the bottom of the heap and owned nothing were still by her side. Those were the ones she trusted.

Attitudes mellowed towards her recently when she'd been enraged after hearing about a local baker who was capitalising on the shortage of supplies by charging extortionate prices for his bread. Some of the worst off were reduced to sharing a loaf of bread.

She, and Mary and Bella, had marched into the city and joined in the storming of the bakery. The protesting baker and his greedy wife were held - captive but unharmed - until all their fresh bread had been distributed, everyone paying a fair price for what they took.

The militant women were greeted with cheers and acclaim by those who witnessed their action and from that day forward two things changed; the mortified baker charged a fair price for his goods and local people were not so quick to shun Ruby when she entered a public space.

She understood the feeling of powerlessness and shame that poverty brought, having experienced the same desperation herself, and wanted to help. She offered a plain cooked meal in exchange for a few hours work to any family man without gainful employment.

She couldn't afford to pay, but she could feed them if they would work.

And work they did, her gardens were scrubbed, buffed and painted to a gloss. Every evening a ragged army of men could be seen heading away from their days work carrying a pail containing hot food for his entire family. She'd helped ordinary men maintain their dignity and they wouldn't forget.

She'd never strived for acceptance, content with her solitary life but lately she was starting to wonder what she had been missing.

And now here she was, breathless from dancing and happily mingling with the crowd, exchanging jests with local families, sharing tankards of strong beer and hunks of fragrant bread.

She danced on, stopping only when she could dance no more. She glanced down at the gown she wore. The narrow column of white muslin with the pretty pink ribbon that gripped her under the bust had been crisp and fresh this morning, the stiches of golden thread had shimmered in the sun. Now it hung limp, smudged and grubby, it had barely lasted the day and wouldn't be fit for another.

She smiled ruefully at Mary who appeared to have read her mind. They linked arms and watched Bella flirt and dance about, crackling with energy and howling with laughter.

She rejected the latest fashion for being dull and dowdy and was resplendent in a tight red plush gown that enhanced her voluptuous figure and suited the flamboyant nature that neither marriage nor widowhood had managed to subdue.

She'd been dancing and fooling non-stop and her face was reddened while her magnificently unrestrained breasts were exciting a certain amount of attention of their own. A couple of young boys kept their eyes on her and held their breath, hoping against hope...

A cry rang out and the crowd turned and watched the lone horseman gallop from St Johns toward the bridge. 'He's here!' The horseman cried. 'He's here!'

All Saints church bells tolled, alerting the nearby churches who were ready to set off their own bells until a chain of chimes circled the city and Worcester heralded their triumphant hero.

At an early hour on Friday morning, intelligence was received in this City of Worcester that the definitive treaty of peace with France had been received in London.

This statement was further confirmed by the London coach to this City, and in consequence immense crowds assembled at various points to witness the arrival of the mail which was brought in upon the joyous occasion in great style, much to the credit of Mr Jones, the coach contractor.

(Copyright and courtesy of the Worcester News)

CHAPTER FOUR

The ground vibrated as the canons discharged, the bridge trembled, and the church towers swayed, sending birds up and squawking.

'Christ, I hope this fucking bridge holds,' Mary moaned. Eyes squeezed shut and fingers gripped around Ruby's wrist so hard she winced.

Emotions overflowed, men roared and stamped their feet, women screamed or fainted, and children layered on howls of distress which continued until an approaching pall of dust, accompanied by the drum of hooves, thrilled them into silence.

An elegant carriage came into view and the band struck up a march, a signal for thirty selected men to step forward and meet it.

The carriage halted, and the nations hero stepped down. Admiral Nelson smiled and bowed, a real flesh and blood man, rather than the familiar impression on a sheet of paper that was all they'd previously seen of him.

He stood unflinching as he was engulfed by wall of cheering. He bowed to the left, then to the right, sweeping off his hat and whirling it above his head. Clearly as delighted by his welcome as the congregation was with him.

England's greatest hero, a near mythical figure, stood on Worcester bridge and the citizens could not be prouder. They waved their flags until their arms ached, giving the great man his due.

'Bleeding hell, he's shorter than I expected him to be,' Bella declared to muffled laughter. She raised her hands in disbelief, slightly put out.

'No. Really, I'd imagined him to be a much bigger fellow somehow!'

The notorious Lady Hamilton was handed from the carriage to stand beside her man. She was glorious and gracious as she waved and smiled and took great care not to stand in front of their hero. Barely a week passed when she was not referred to in the newspapers, the fascination about what she wore, what she ate, what colour her horses were, was never ending and no detail went unreported.

Ruby's delight at being so close to this fabulous woman, whose wicked exploits had kept England agog, was overwhelming. She scrutinised her posture, her dress and her dainty silver slippers and was not disappointed. Emma Hamilton was as perfect as legend had led her to suppose.

Ruby had amused herself for years by noting the parallels in their lives. They were the same age and both low born, they had the nerve to seize every opportunity and make something of it. They lived as they saw fit and held their heads high and their gaze steady. Others saw scandal, but they were unapologetic.

In fact, she thought, the only difference between them was that Emma Hamilton endured the merciless glare of the nation's probing eyes, whilst she'd only had to deal with those in Worcester.

The onlookers watched as the advance party of men demonstrated what they'd rehearsed endlessly for. The sweating horses were unhitched, and the thirty men took their places. Nelson and Emma were handed back into the horseless carriage and the men bent, tensed, and towed them slowly across the bridge and up into the centre of the city. A gesture of respect to the man who had brought an end to the French threat.

The parade advanced, stopping every few yards to enable everyone to get close to him and to allow him to admire the tributes, in the shape of blue and gold flags, pennants and ribbons that decorated the frontage of every shop, house and inn along the route.

The three women linked arms and ambled slowly behind, waving to friends and accepting drinks as they went. Footsore but deeply content.

'As I said, he's only a little fellow up close, but I still would, given the chance! Wo, ho, Horatio.' Bella sang out, setting of a chorus.

Stories were spreading like wildfire. Someone said Nelson had stopped and shaken his hands, another swore he clapped him on the shoulder and someone else's child had had his chin tickled. The more ale they drank, the wilder the stories became.

The parade halted at the Hop Pole Inn, their ultimate destination. A grand banquet was to be followed by endless speeches from the city's dignitaries, all of whom would trample over one another to get close to the great man.

Those without an invitation considered themselves the lucky ones. A street party with a hog roast and unlimited ale, followed by a sing song and some dancing would be a barrel load more fun than the tedium lined up for poor old Nelson.

Stalls were quickly set up and braziers crackled and glowed down the length of the track. Ruby danced on, tired feet forgotten.

Every so often Nelson stepped out onto the balcony to wave to the crowd outside, who begged and gestured for him to come down and join them. He laughed but shook his head and, with another wave, went back inside.

'Poor bugger probably wants to sleep but our noise won't let him.' Bella laughed. 'When we sleep he'll sleep.'

Ruby yawned. 'That's now for me. Let's call it a night. We'll be back here first thing and we shan't miss anything but the fighting if we slip away now.'

'Another hour or so Rube.' Bella pleaded.

Ruby shook her head. 'You stay if you want to. I need to sleep, I want to be back here first thing to see them walk through town and then I'll be racing around the gardens all afternoon.' She stifled a yawn. 'Sorry love, you're on your own.'

Mary agreed. 'C'mon Bella, you're looking a bit rough around the edges, let's leave the partying to young ones.'

'Bitch.' Bella grinned as Mary took one arm and Ruby the other.

They walked, content with their day but a little wistful. Partying all night long had been their way of life and it rankled to accept that if they tried that now, they'd be good for nothing the following day.

The brave avenger of his country's wrongs was greeted by joyous peels of church bells and several discharges of cannon and the various testimonies of esteem and respect continued till night had completely drawn her sable mantle o'er the scene.
(Copyright and courtesy of the Worcester News)

CHAPTER FIVE

Early next morning Ruby and Mary walked briskly towards the Hop Pole, Bella having cried off.

'Met a fellow, no doubt.'

They picked their way over or around the die-hards. Some feebly waving an empty jug or bottle around, some muttering a song, a great many more snoring where they'd fallen. A few hardy souls were attempting to continue the party and Ruby cried with laughter as a frustrated housewife put an end to their noise with well-aimed bucket of stinking slops.

A considerably smaller and more subdued gathering waited for Nelson and Emma to appear, buzzing with conversations about the night before, intending to follow their scheduled promenade through the city to the porcelain factory where they would tour the works, meet some of the artists, and then have a luncheon.

'Oh, just look at her, isn't she a picture?'

Mary sniffed. 'She's pretty enough I suppose.'

Ruby laughed and squeezed her shoulders. 'Don't be grumpy.'

They rested on the banks of the river, dozing and drifting until a rumble rippled through. Nelson had been delighted with the factory and enjoyed his luncheon. So happy was he, he'd ordered a dinner service of a hundred pieces, guaranteeing work for at least a year.

Applause for him and his generosity rocked the Guild Hall where he was granted the freedom of the city.

'Not that we'd turn him away if he was to come back any time soon.' Ruby declared.

Nelson stepped out into public view, whirled his hat and bowed to the cheering crowd before stepping up into his carriage.

He and Worcester made their fond farewells.

The Indian Juggler who has astonished audiences nation-wide and here in Worcester by his dangerous feat of passing a drawn sword down to his stomach, has unfortunately fallen sacrifice to his presumption. (Copyright and courtesy of the Worcester News)

CHAPTER SIX

Ruby tore her eyes from the departing carriage and resolutely turned her attention back to her own business.

'That's it then. Back to work.'

She'd gambled that people who had travelled to see Nelson would want to stay and rest for a while and perhaps sample what else was at their disposal before returning to the daily drudge.

Ruby's people had done their level best, while out mingling and partying, to spread the word that Sansome Springs would be opening later that afternoon, a shady and cool paradise where they could rest and recover from the celebrations. Later they could try the finest hot supper in town, along with music, dancing and a host of other entertainments. There would be no limits on the fun to be had.

She'd lost a little ground yesterday, but she'd make up for it today. A whisper that a surprise guest would be in attendance circulated and, although it was assumed this was nonsense designed to draw in a greater crowd, it was acknowledged that at Sansome Springs anything could, and frequently did, occur.

Who'd risk missing out? Surprise guest or not there would be plenty to see and do, and the food guaranteed that no visit was ever a disappointment.

Ruby estimated she had about four hours before a crowd of any decent number gathered. There'd be stragglers drifting along before then, but entertaining the masses was her business. She'd laid her plans weeks ago and had everything in place, but still she'd double check everything.

She had good people working for her but occasionally one of them tried to introduce something she'd not bargained for and she had to be quick to jump on that kind of thing. Her world would be run her way. Her gardens were a success because of her and her passion and no-one made any changes but her.

There were no such incidents for her to deal with today though and so, once she had satisfied herself that everything humanly possible had been done to create a magical and successful night, she wandered aimlessly and reflected on an awkward situation that she could no longer ignore.

She been determined not to be distracted from this event, but first thing tomorrow, she had a problem to resolve.

The new comedy of the School for Scandal was performed in Worcester by Messrs Crump and Chamberlain's company to very brilliant and crowded houses. From the attention the performers gave to their several parts, as well as the necessary decoration to the stage by the managers, there is no doubt of its still meeting with general approbation and encouragement. (Copyright and courtesy of the Worcester News)

CHAPTER SEVEN

Barnabus Peek was the outstanding cook who had turned the kitchens of Sansome Springs into the talk of the Midlands. He was a new addition to Ruby's workforce and came highly recommended, having learned all he knew from Liz Porter, an old friend who kept a London inn.

She'd taken him on and, from a professional point of view, didn't regret it. He'd revolutionised her menu, having learned his craft in a kitchen that had to satisfy the pickiest London customers. He was steadily introducing her and her visitors to foods they'd never previously enjoyed.

They'd worked together happily for several months until he made an idiot of himself and cast a shadow where there had been none. She was furious with herself for being so slow on the uptake. If she'd been paying attention she could have nipped it in the bud before it became an issue.

She didn't know when it began but was thrown into a panic one lunch time when his intent became clear. Her habit was to live simply and eat sparingly, something she'd learned from Ma. For her mid-day break she'd take a little of whatever was available and tuck herself away in a neglected little alcove that she considered her thinking space.

She'd been horrified to find her sanctuary had been invaded and messed about with. The floor had been freshly swept and there were flowers on the table. He'd set out a meal for her, *with silverware* and she was livid.

'This is wasted on me, it's not what you're paid for and I want no more of it.' She took his elbow and prepared to eject him from her space.

He grasped her hand and, before she realised what was happening, declared his admiration and respect for her and asked her to be his wife.

'What are you talking about? I … no. No!' She pressed her hands on his chest and pushed him away.

He clasped one of her hands. 'I'm sorry, I took you by surprise, don't refuse me, I can wait.'

She shook him off angrily. 'I've never heard anything so ridiculous, we barely know each other and if we did, you'd know I'm not a marrying kind of woman. For heaven sake, what were you thinking?'

He was shocked and offended. His only previous experience of women was his relationship with darling Liz, who'd spent her entire adult life longing to be wed. Years of listening to Liz chatter about her hopes and dreams had taught him that marriage was something all women wanted.

He thought he was doing Ruby a favour and was appalled at her reaction.

She was furious, a decent working relationship was wrecked by a stupid man who hadn't the sense he'd been born with. He was the best cook she'd ever had, the staff flourished under his guidance and his food was second to none, but he had to ruin it.

And, instead of backing off to lick his wounds he'd convinced himself that she'd turned him down because she'd been taken by surprise. He'd tried to woo her. Little gifts or a note would appear on her table, sometimes he'd surprise her with a visit when he knew she was alone.

He wanted a reason, there was no other suitor in sight, he was a good prospect, what was she waiting for?

She didn't want him picking away at her life, her reasons were her business. She lived without shame but preferred not to be the subject of gossip it. Her living arrangements with Mary, if they became known, could give rise to the kind of tittle tattle she'd no taste for.

Of all the things in life Ruby desired, a husband was not one. She could name half dozen women desperate for a man, why couldn't he have picked one of them? She wanted him running her kitchens and providing first class food. He had a home and a good job, why couldn't that be enough?

His father, Rufus, scratched a scant living moving from town to town selling anything he could buy cheaply enough. It was a desperate hand-to-mouth existence with little cheer.

Seth Porter had discovered Rufus sleeping in their stable and had been about to throw him out with a black eye for his cheek when he noticed the small, shivering boy cowering behind some grain barrels. Seth's bluff and bluster deserted him, and he brought them into his kitchen to feed them as he heard their story.

Rufus met Sarah on his first day in town and they'd liked each other enough to convince him to stay for a few weeks. Their courtship continued until her family found out what was going on and forbade her to have anything to do with a penniless drifter.

The two were gone before daylight. They slept in barns or under hayricks and he taught her his trade. Sometimes they bought their food; more often they stole it. A chicken here, a handful of eggs there, perhaps a pie a woman had left on a sill to cool. They were young and healthy and so in love that it didn't matter if they had to cuddle up together wrapped in his cloak to sleep under a hedge.

Love cooled with the seasons. Cold nights and wet days took their toll. Long, loving summer nights had to be paid for. Sarah became unwell, sickly and lethargic. Life on the road with insufficient food, a lack of sleep and long days walking were her undoing. She died within days of giving birth to Barnabus.

Rough, tough Seth found himself wanting to help. He could do nothing for Rufus but offered to give the little boy a home and a trade, an offer that was rapidly accepted. Rufus loved his son but taking responsibility for another human being was something he was ill equipped for. He was heartbroken that Sarah had died, and he'd never forgive himself. Life had not turned out the way he hoped, and he was defeated. His haste to leave the care of his child with someone else was almost unseemly.

Yet the boy adapted to his new circumstances quickly, he'd known nothing but cold and hunger and this new situation was heaven. He had clothes that were warm and fitted him and he had his own bed; the same one every night! He was given hot food twice a day and plenty of ale to drink. For weeks he crept about in silence hoping that they wouldn't realise how much he was eating and throw him out.

He answered when spoken to but otherwise remained silent, so anxious was he to cause no trouble and be removed. He watched everyone and learned how the business worked and then he naturally began to do the jobs that needed to be done almost before Seth realised. Through his quick brain and willing heart, he carved out a secure place at the inn.

Seth worried occasionally that the silent child might be a dullard, but Liz was confident he'd come around sooner or later. She told her father to leave him alone until he'd put some weight on and gained a little strength, she knew the boy in him would come out one day.

Seth treated him exactly as he'd treated Liz as a girl, lessons in the morning and work in the kitchen in the afternoons and evenings. He adapted well to the ebb and flow of too much work, and then too little. He learned to call Seth uncle and Liz cousin and became invaluable to their business.

He paid close attention to the cook and began to bake for pleasure after completing his given work of cleaning out the stables and fetching and carrying. This left Seth and Liz free to cater to their customers knowing that everything behind the scenes was running as it should.

Seth died eighteen months ago and left Liz in a turmoil of mixed emotions. She grieved for her father while acknowledging that with him gone, she'd attract a husband. Men that were afraid of her sharp tongue and biting wit would find her easier to bear as the owner of a prosperous inn.

She'd long accepted she was no beauty, but she'd always been confident that her day would come. She took her time, and had a lot of fun selecting her groom, and when she was good and ready a wedding took place.

She'd been his only female friend and was almost a sister to him, he was privy to her dreams and he knew how desperately she had longed for a husband, he shared her unbridled joy when she accepted Hugo's proposal.

He was a decent man who had a hundred and one ideas to upgrade the place he was now master of and, although nothing was said, it was time for Barnabus to move on. There was room for only one man in Liz's inn.

He was confident in his skills and never doubted they would guarantee him a place wherever he chose to go. Liz's advised him to make for Worcester, she and Ruby were friends and might give him a chance. Having nowhere else to go, he followed her advice.

Meeting Ruby had affected him deeply. She was determined and passionate about everything she turned her hand to and he found that exciting. He was soon caught up in her grand ideas and began to imagine life as her partner.

He could be Hugo to her Liz. He could make a difference here, put down his own roots. Together they would be invincible! These pleasure gardens rivalled anything he'd ever seen in London and the entertainments she offered were truly first class, but what had impressed him the most was her unabashed thirst for making a healthy profit and then quietly spending half of it educating and helping those who had nothing. He could love a woman like that.

And he'd mucked it up.

He watched as his trainees demonstrated that everything he'd taught them was paying off and the extravaganza that Ruby had planned for tonight would be well catered for. He thanked his stars for them because he knew he wasn't doing his best work.

He'd made a complete fool of himself and then, rather than have the sense to leave things alone he'd compounded his error. He had no idea how to put things back onto an even keel.

They'd got on so well together from the very first, often seeming to know what the other was thinking, she could propose an idea, he could visualise what she described and build on her original idea, she would agree and then elaborate. They'd been able to argue, debate and finish a meeting laughing together.

He'd fallen under her spell and assumed that his feelings were reciprocated. They were close enough in age, he was a little younger but not too much, they had no entanglements and enjoyed being together. What could be more natural than to combine their talents?

This evenings celebration would go ahead as planned but then, first thing tomorrow morning he'd have to leave this magical place.

*We are happy to learn that it is intended to open a Soup
Shop in this city for the benefit of the labouring classes,
and that the gentlemen who kindly undertook its
management on former occasions, are again making
preparations for that benevolent purpose.
(Copyright and courtesy of the Worcester News)*

CHAPTER EIGHT

Richard Morgan strode across the courtyard with a rare spring in his step. He'd spent the day verifying that the newspaper coverage of Nelson's visit was up to date and suitably reverent. Having been among the dignitaries invited to dine at the Hop Pole and meet the man, he wanted to be sure this fact was given prominence in the report.

'Have you spoken to Ruby yet?' His wife's hectoring voice slammed into him as he entered his house and dashed away the foolish hope he'd had for a relaxing evening. Elizabeth was a master at sucking any pleasure there was to be had from his life and experience told him this no more than a warning shot.

'Today? Truly my dear, your sense of time and place are quite ridiculous.' She drove him mad and he retaliated with pomposity, knowing that infuriated her. 'You've just dined with the saviour of England and still you complain?'

She stepped forward to check that the door was closed, and his heart sank. She had a bee in her bonnet and the barrage of complaints would escalate in pitch and frequency until she achieved her aim.

He sighed, overwhelmed with his various burdens of trying to please his wife, oversee the newspaper, feed his children and avoid his mother.

In principle he agreed with Elizabeth's argument that it was time for a clear line of separation between himself and Ruby. The newspaper should be transferred to him, it was what he'd been trained for and yes, they'd waited long enough.

Raising the matter with Ruby was the tricky thing. A confrontation could cost him his position and, given the wicked temper he'd inherited from her, a clash of wills was inevitable. If he didn't rock the boat, he'd inherit in the end, so why risk an upset?

The mother - son relationship was complicated, he lurched between hating her, despising her, and wishing he was more like her. They skirted around one another like wild cats, hissing and spitting, neither knowing how to be. They'd often reached a point of harmony, but only fleetingly, it took very little to offend or irritate one or other of them.

Nowadays she left him alone to do his job and he was loath to do anything that would fire up her interest in him and his family or draw attention to his daily doings. He simply had no idea how to manage his mother and so he followed the easier path of letting things lie.

But Elizabeth couldn't do that, she adored the dinners and galas they were invited to because Richard was the steward of the newspaper. Her argument was simple, if he was the *owner*, it would be she issuing the invitations and sitting at the top table. All that stood in the way of her ambition was Ruby.

And as if that wasn't enough to drive her to fury, her own children adored their grandmother and for the life of her she couldn't see why. If she could, she'd sever all relations with Ruby, and her frustration evident.

The fight had to be shelved for now though, shrieks and giggles announced their children, racing to greet their father. Eliza, Emily and Georgiana dragged, hauled and pushed, baby Thomas into the room and both parents smiled.

Elizabeth loved her children wholeheartedly and would do anything before letting them discover their parents were at odds. Richard knew she'd contain her venomous spite until later, for now she'd bless them all with sweetness.

Peace reigned, though it would be short lived. Their marriage was making neither of them happy and, although they both tried hard at times, life was becoming ever more unpleasant as they faced their unhappiness.

Elizabeth's parents, Mr and Mrs Trovel had been delighted when six years passed after the birth of a son, their tenth child. Confident her childbearing years were safely behind her, her husband become once more the energetic and attentive lover she'd loved before a baby a year dampened her ardour.

Elizabeth's arrival was a shocking affront to them both. Mama removed herself to a bedroom on a different floor and Papa's dreams of reducing his workload crumbled to dust.

Elizabeth realised at a very young age that she was neither special nor important, rather a nuisance, a mistake. She wore clothes that had been worn by at least three others before her, she played with toys that had been broken and mended on countless occasions and had never had a playmate to call her own. Her brothers and sisters were too grown up to give her little more than a pat on the head when they saw her, while her parents did their best to ignore her.

She dreamed of having new things, things that had never belonged to anyone else. She'd have lots of children and they'd love her above all others. She'd need a husband and she pictured a man like Papa, at work from dawn until dusk, leaving the home to his wife and offering nothing in the way of criticism, and providing her with a position in society, a carriage, a large staff, and a grand house.

There was no end to Elizabeth's girlish ambitions and when she met the unhappy son of the owner of the local newspaper she found her heart's desire. A man who needed her to guide him.

He was grieving for his twin and almost estranged from his mother and he leaned on her gratefully. As she took care of everything he realised only Elizabeth could make the world endurable. He wanted to be left alone and she saw to it that he was. Her cool practicality calmed his turmoil and he mistook gratitude for love.

The birth of Eliza transformed Elizabeth into a doting mother and a demanding wife. She was finished with nursing him, now it was time for him to look after her and their baby. He was unequal to the task.

Her hysterical demands for a suitable family home, rather than the cottage they shared with Ann, drove him to appeal to Ruby who stepped in and built the solid house they now inhabited.

This may well have been what hardened Elizabeth's attitude. The sturdy new house was build facing the newspaper office and Ruby retained ownership. Elizabeth was distraught and increased her campaign to seize the newspaper from Ruby. Barely a day had passed in the years since that she had not gone on the attack.

Richard smiled at the antics of his children while his mind toyed with this latest argument. If he was the owner he wouldn't be required to give Ruby a monthly financial report, or to grovel and justify every penny if he needed a lump sum for something, both of which humiliated him to the point of sickness. He'd be free to make the decisions and be answerable to no-one. He'd direct things the way he wanted them to go. He could build a house in the city.

But he wouldn't, the thought of all that responsibility paralysed him. He didn't care about the business, it was an income, and an irritation. A constant reminder that no matter what he did Ruby was there, looking over his shoulder and seeing only disappointment.

His complex feelings for her had evolved as he matured. As a boy, he'd idolised her. She taught him everything he knew from how to read and write through to doing what was right for you, even though the world might say you were wrong.

She was distant, but kind, and preached that hard work and paying one's own way was crucial, no-one should ever be ashamed of what they did to earn a living provided it didn't hurt anyone else.

'Be proud of who you are and where you came from and you'll never need to lie or apologise for anything.'

He was twenty years old when he learned that every word she'd uttered had been a lie. It knocked his world off kilter and from that day forward he no longer knew what to do or who to trust.

He discovered a twin he'd known nothing about and they quickly established a brotherly rapport and, along the way, helped the other forgive Ruby for their fractured childhood.

But it was a surface forgiveness, he couldn't get past the knowledge that for twenty years she'd pretended to be his aunt, not his mother, and kept his brother away from him. She was unnatural.

When Tom died in a fire, Richard gave up on life. That was when Elizabeth rescued him.

And now, he could quite cheerfully walk away from the lot of them.

Yesterday between three and four in the afternoon, his Royal Highness the Duke of York arrived at the Hop Pole Inn, Worcester where he dined before leaving the city. The Mayor, as soon as possible, waited on His Highness, was received in a very courteous manner and had the honour of kissing His Royal Highness's hand. (Copyright and courtesy of the Worcester News)

CHAPTER NINE

Ellie sat in her neat little parlour and scanned the newspaper for coverage of Nelson's visit, which she'd been obliged to miss, due to the ghastly bruising on her face. Shame kept her indoors.

After reading about the celebrations and the order of a dinner service that would give work to half the city she flicked on to see if there was any mention of Sansome Springs. She missed seeing her sister but discouraged her from visiting, wanting to keep the truth about her marital woes private.

Harold had taken against her twin and would cause a scene if he found her in his house, another reason to keep her away.

Ellie admired Ruby, she'd achieved exactly what she wanted in her life and bowed to no-one, she had an abundance of confidence and positively delighted in proving her critics wrong. She'd often accused Ellie of lacking backbone.

Ellie was a born pleaser, losing sleep if anyone thought badly of her. She required the approval of others to erase her own self-doubt. She'd dearly wanted her own home and a husband to take care of her and jumped into marriage at the first offer. The reality of marriage was not what she'd dreamed of, Harold was unkind and quick to anger, certain that others were against him. He complained of being slighted by one person or another daily. She'd learned to be cautious, never quite knowing what could tip his bad mood over into ugliness.

'I see you've read the reports surrounding your sister's latest ambitions.' His voice boomed out and she flinched, not realising he was in the house.

Ellie folded the newspaper and handed it to him with a smile. 'I thought you were out dear, let me send for some tea.'

'I don't want tea, I want my newspaper!' He snatched it from her hands and left the room.

She'd be punished for reading it before him, he generally handed it to her when he'd finished with it, but she hadn't expected him home this evening and broke the rule. It would be worse because he'd caught her reading about Ruby.

She glanced around the room quickly for anything jarring that she should clear away, it was impossible to imagine what might upset him when he was in one of his moods. He'd return in moment or two, when he wanted to fight he'd keep on until she said something to enrage him, which justified him losing control.

Ellie was a bright woman who knew she'd made a dreadful, irreversible mistake. One that she had to find a way to make tolerable.

The uncertainty stretched her nerves, he was skilled at keeping her on a knife edge and could go for days before exploding in anger. And yet, this dreadful separation he had created between her and Ruby hurt her far more than his anger.

Having been estranged as children they re-united as young women. Ellie had been without work or a home and Ruby came to the rescue, helping her become known professionally as Madame Eloise in which persona she passed beauty tips to ladies and their maids.

The sisters met regularly in private, carefully keeping their public lives separate, knowing that Ruby's reputation wouldn't be appreciated by the clients of Madame Eloise.

The salon was situated in the best part of town and Ellie was thrilled to be befriended by her neighbours. Very soon she and Clara began taking tea together once a week and their friendship developed although Ellie never let it slip that in her past she'd have been a maid to a woman like Clara. When Clara became desperately ill, Ellie was the first to know, Harold the second.

Throughout her friend's steady decline Ellie visited most days to help the family. Clara was mother to two small sons who were both confused and frightened by their mother's illness. Ellie was moved by their distress and did all she could to comfort them.

Clara passed away and, almost without realising it, Ellie became a substitute mother. Her own sadness eased as she showered the sad little boys with all the love she could, her dormant mothering instincts rushing to the fore.

The widower saw that she was devoted to his boys and decided she'd make an ideal second wife. He ran a demanding business and would find it impossible to bring up the boys alone. Ellie suited his needs. She was past the first flush of youth, being older than him by a good ten years, which reduced the chances of her having her own children but increased the likelihood of her gratitude for being rescued from spinsterhood. He wondered how she might demonstrate her appreciation.

After a decent period of mourning they quietly married. He'd provided a mother for his children, a housekeeper for himself, and gained control of his wife's assets into the bargain.

In the early days he left the business of Madame Eloise well alone, concentrating all his attention on teaching Ellie what he required of a wife.

The household staff changed, a new cook was brought in, a dry, thin woman who deferred to him but was almost dismissive of Ellie. A young man came to help with a variety of duties around the home and there was no mistaking his disdain for Ellie.

Harold laughed at her concern, insisting their disrespect was all in her imagination, she worried about slights that simply did not exist. 'It's because you're unused to servants. You pay them too much attention, ignore them.'

Ellie did her best and devoted herself to the boys, Samuel and Simon, who had accepted her as their mother very quickly and were a joy to be with.

Meanwhile Harold quietly assessed the sums of money that rolled into the coffers of Madame Eloise and bided his time. One night, having asserted himself on the tender body of his inexperienced wife, he announced his plans.

'I've considered our business situation and have decided our respective shops should become one. I've engaged Miller to come tomorrow and begin the work.'

She gasped, though he ignored her entirely.

'There's a demand from the wives of my customers for the services you provide and I'm certain you could recommend my products to your ladies. Females could wander from one side to the other unimpeded.'

She shook her head unable to mask her feelings. 'Oh no, that would be a dreadful error. Exclusivity and discretion are the reasons ladies use my services. I can't allow uninvited people to simply wander through at will. Madame Eloise is not a shop!'

His jaw clenched and in an instant his hand was at her throat and she was pinned against the wall, struggling for breath.

'Must I remind you that what *was* yours is now mine and I'll do as I see fit. A *shop* was good enough for Clara and it will be for you. You dare to look down your nose at me, but you're my wife and you *will* support my plans.'

He loosened his grip and she dropped to her knees.

'The builder will begin the work tomorrow, it is arranged.'

Her voice shook but she knew she had to speak. 'You must consult Ruby.'

He laughed. 'Why on earth would I consult *your* sister about *my* affairs?'

'Because Ruby owns Madame Eloise.'

The abuse he subjected her to that night confined her to bed for three days. Madame Eloise was not referred to again.

But Harold had friends, powerful men who could steer him in the right direction and he consulted them. If he could demonstrate that he'd been tricked, then surely some pressure could be brought to bear, if that failed then wouldn't a truly caring sister be prevailed upon to gift the business to a newly-wed couple in celebration of their union?

Ruby *was* a caring sister who was sharp enough to understand that her sister's future was not as secure now as it had been. When approached by his agents, she flatly refused to surrender ownership of her business, assuring them that Ellie could continue to act as Madame Eloise and receive a share of the income for as long as she pleased but ownership would never transfer from her own hands.

From that moment on Ellie was treated as a housemaid at best and a whore at worst. Nothing she did was right, and she became adept a hiding her bruises.

He disappeared for days on end, returning only to open his shop and then leaving when he closed. She cherished those nights and didn't concern herself with his whereabouts.

Hearing his footsteps outside the door and she straightened up to face him. He'd worked himself up into a rage which meant his violence would almost certainly end with a sexual assault. The fact that he derived so much pleasure from these perversions sickened her.

Harold seethed with frustration. Not only did Ellie bring nothing of value into the marriage, she'd caused him to be related to the most disreputable woman in the city. She was known to associate with the lowest of the low and no matter what glossy veneer was erected by those it suited, she was a filthy harlot and ever would be to his mind.

The two were fixed in an intolerable situation. His anger had not abated, in fact it had worsened as he made it his business to learn all he could about his new sister-in-law whilst plotting his revenge.

On Sunday the improvements at St Andrew's Church, Worcester were commenced upon by the first stone being laid by the Right Worshipful the Mayor, H. Rogers. (Copyright and courtesy of the Worcester News)

CHAPTER TEN

Half a dozen burly men held braziers aloft helping to guide people into Sansome Springs.

Foot passengers caught up with coaches and carriages that had breezed past them on track and happily dodged around the blocked traffic to get in front, laughing at the impotent rage of the trapped drivers who dished out abuse but were unable to move forward or back.

The conditions of the tracks and the volume of vehicles trying to navigate them made travelling on the waterways an attractive option. The two landing stages that Ruby had built had paid for themselves a dozen times over. Several barges lined up, laden with party-goers all raring to disembark and join the fun.

Ruby typically spent her evenings in the shadows gauging the reaction of her visitors, aware that she had to keep her entertainment fresh and exciting. She'd stroll arm in arm with Bella or Mary and pass unnoticed.

'These out of towners are filling the place up nicely.' Bella sighed happily.

Ruby nodded. 'I was confident of a good turn-out, but I'm hoping some of them will want to come back, so I've got to keep my eyes open.'

Pretty lights were strung from the trees, flattering on older skin and offering plenty of shadows for those who preferred privacy. The air of romance and excitement that obscurity hinted at was beyond price.

A thrill of pent up expectation passed through the crowd. The respectful behaviour that they'd displayed in honour of their hero was not required out here.

In addition to the usual entertainments were barrows laden with trinkets decorated to commemorate the occasion and already people were drinking from tankards they'd just purchased.

Bright blue banners and flags fluttered at every turn, the golden anchors glittering with reflected light.

'They're falling over themselves to spend their money, just look at them.' Bella pointed to the giggling girls clustered around the man selling clips and pins in the shapes of ships or anchors and even cannons.

'It doesn't hurt that he's best looking lad I could find.' Ruby knew a pretty face could sell anything.

As the buying frenzy slowed so the music sped up and dancing began. Staff inconspicuously spread out chairs in preparation for when the dancers tired in an hour or so, at which time a variety show was planned.

'Who have you got on tonight then?'

'Mary Grace, she's done a stint in Cheltenham but never in Worcester. She's a pretty little thing, they'll love her.'

They did. They also liked the bawdy poetry recital that followed her sweetly sentimental act.

Having learned how quickly people grew bored, Ruby was constantly seeking the new or unusual. She also ensured there were other, more specialised attractions available for those keen to venture away from the mainstream.

Players, singers and acrobats performed whenever there was a group in search of something a little more risqué. The sounds of laughter and cries of admiration warmed her heart.

'Come this way, I've got something a bit special lined up.' Ruby pulled Bella away from the magician and around to a secluded clearing. 'I want to see how it goes down.'

As a rule, throughout the course of an evening she overheard enough to be armed with information to plan a whole season of events. She took risks and had no fear of causing offence, knowing a sense of shock or outrage guaranteed a bigger crowd the following night.

She and Bella sat and watched a trio of players re-enact a piece of gossip that had been swirling around concerning the arrangement of Nelson, Emma Hamilton and her breathtakingly tolerant husband, Lord Hamilton.

It was common knowledge that the three shared a home and the exact nature of their relationship gave the country something delicious to speculate on.

As the crowd watching the sketch roared out their encouragement to the players she smiled with satisfaction and squeezed Bella's hand. 'Go on off and have some fun, it's bed time for me.'

Ruby slept through the stunning fireworks and music show that always closed the evening's entertainment.

At one point she sleepily turned over and reached out her hand, smiling as Mary kissed it.

On Saturday last, an inquest was held at the Crown Inn, Droitwich, near this city by Mr Hill, coroner, on the body of William Smith, hairdresser of the Tything, Worcester, who on Thursday night, being in a state of intoxication, walked into the pool near the home of H Wakeman Esq. at Perdiswell Hall and was drowned. (Copyright and courtesy of the Worcester News)

CHAPTER ELEVEN

'Ellie's in a jam and Ruby's dug her heels in. I thought I might take a walk over to The Foregate and have a bit of a nosey around. Come with me?' Mary said.

'Not a bloody chance. Leave it alone, it's her business. I tried to talk to her the other day and she'll have none of it.'

Mary shook her head. 'She's worried to death, I can tell. That selfish cat needs to see sense. I'm going today.'

Bella put her hands on her hips. 'Well, you'll go on your bloody own. You might be willing to manage Ruby and her moods, but I'm not.'

Mary stepped out briskly, before she had second thoughts. If she got on with it, she'd be home before she was missed and no-one any wiser. Her confidence didn't desert her until she stepped through the lobby of Madame Eloise.

A maid smiled a greeting and Mary panicked and muttered a false name. Ruby guarded her privacy fiercely, how the hell did she think she could she mend whatever had torn the twins apart and not lose her own life?

Just as she decided to make a run for it, the plush red curtains parted to admit Hannah and Mary had to brazen it out.

'I was hoping for a little time with Ellie,' she said crisply.

'You know full well she is Madame Eloise here, and anyway she's not free to see you today.' Hannah said.

'I didn't give my real name, so she doesn't even know it's me.' Mary knew this chit of old and wouldn't be taking any nonsense from her.

Hannah lips curved, though it couldn't be called a smile. 'Our clients rarely give their real name Mary. Madame Eloise is not available to anyone, and I have a full day ahead, so why don't you tell me what you want, and we can both get on?'

Mary pulled her shoulders back and was a little surprised to see Hannah stiffen her own spine, she wasn't going to back down as easily as she'd imagined.

'For a start you can take that snippy tone from your voice. We come from the same place my girl. Now, I'm staying until I get to the bottom of what's wrong between Ellie and Ruby. I'm worried, and if you had a spark of loyalty you would be too. Let me remind you that neither you, nor Ellie, would be living the lives you live now if not for Ruby.'

Hannah looked at her sharply. 'Any debt I owe has been repaid in hard work. Ellie's my boss and if she wants privacy then she'll have it.'

Mary scowled. 'Your debt will never be paid, you were in trouble and Ruby saved you, gave you a home and decent work. Where do you think you'd be without her? She lifted you from disgrace and I shan't forget your disloyalty to her today.'

Hannah's face lost all colour as she nervously paced the room, straightening a drape and moving a vase. 'Have a heart Mary, no-one can serve two mistresses. What do you expect from me?'

'Don't play dumb. You've been around those two long almost long as me and you know there's never been a rift like this. I want to help them, and you should too, are you with me or not?'

Hannah nodded reluctantly.

'Then tell me what you know. What's changed?'

She and Ellie had shared accommodation, and secrets, for many years, but their intimacy was lost when Ellie married and moved into the home next door leaving Hannah's world poorer. The confidences they'd always exchanged stopped abruptly. Hannah felt rejected and her hurt had made her slow to notice that Ellie was not the blushing bride she should be.

All she could tell Mary was what she'd observed recently, but once she'd decided to help, she shared all she knew.

'She was so happy when he proposed, giggling and talking about his boys all day long. But the glow left her quickly. She was quiet, thoughtful, but like I say I didn't think anything of it. I know she thought she was taking another step up and I thought she was pushing me away, for not being good enough.

'They argue mostly at night, I can tell he's not happy with her, but I don't know why. Last week there was note pushed under my door saying she was sick with a fever and I was to manage as best I could alone. He's been in every afternoon since, asking questions about the business, but I haven't seen her.

'I've never known her to stay away for so long, even when Clara was ill she never took her eyes off what was going on here, she loves it that much. Since she got wed, she's a different woman. She won't confide in me, so I don't know what's gone wrong and I feel dreadful, talking about her now.'

Mary told her briskly to stop snivelling and proceeded to tease out every snippet of information she could.

'I often hear her laughing with the boys when he's down in the shop. I wonder if perhaps she's struggling with being a married woman, from what I can make out ...' She blushed scarlet ... 'These walls are that thin.'

'Get on with it.

'It's in the bedroom where the worst of the rows are, and no-one can help her there.' Hannah was tormented by the disloyalty she felt she was showing.

'If you hear her laughing then perhaps there's nothing much wrong. She might be finding life as a newly-wed hard and considering what a prissy so and so she's always been, that's no surprise. Perhaps her virile young husband is teaching her a few life lessons.'

'Oh Mary!'

Subscribers and the public are respectfully informed that the next Card and Dancing Assembly at the Unicorn Inn, Broad Street, Worcester, will be held on Wednesday. (Copyright and courtesy of the Worcester News)

CHAPTER TWELVE

Ruby was unsurprised to find Barnabus in the kitchens, pacing the floor nervously as he waited for her. He looked up at the sound of her footsteps and she saw him swallow.

They spoke in unison, anxious to say their piece and clear the air.

'We must talk, I don't want the awkwardness between us to ...'

'Let me explain myself...'

The resulting jumble of words eased the tension and they both smiled.

'I apologise for the embarrassment I caused you. I truly regret it. I spoke hastily, without thinking. I'll leave for London on the midday coach and you'll have your calm restored.'

'But that's not what I want at all.' She snapped, her irritation flaring up again.

'I wish you would stop trying to think for me, it's pointless and destructive. Sit down and let me tell you what I *do* want from you.'

Over the course of the next hour she told him how much difference he had made to the kitchens, how delighted she was with the quality of food he provided and how highly she valued his opinions.

She described what she wanted to achieve in the future and how she envisaged him playing an important part in that scheme. She had no desire to lose him, simply to put their relationship back on the entirely professional footing they had previously enjoyed.

'I'm not a marrying kind of woman, that's my choice. You are a marrying kind of man and my mistake has been to allow you to bury yourself in the kitchen and see no life outside of work. You're in a strange city where you know no-one. You need friends and a life apart from your work and then you'll meet the right woman.'

His expression confirmed that he had no desire to leave. Worcester suited him. He *was* lonely, but he could cope with that. If Ruby pictured him working alongside her then he'd manage.

'Why don't you select two of your best helpers and teach them what you do? We can get you out in the gardens, meeting and talking to our customers, maybe once or twice a week to begin with. You've achieved great things in here, but I think you'll do as much good out there.'

As she fleshed out what had been a fleeting idea, she became more enthused. 'You can tell me what you think we lack and help me identify weak spots.'

She nodded decisively. 'Yes, another pair of eyes and ears, that what I need from you. What do you think?'

He clasped her hand then pulled back as though it was red hot. 'Sorry. Yes, I think I could do that, certainly I could.'

'And as your face becomes known, you'll meet people and make friends.'

He beamed, he'd been given another chance and he wouldn't spoil it this time. His dream of a future here was restored and if she was generous enough to rise above his foolishness then he'd try to forget it himself.

She'd offered him the chance of a lifetime and he'd be forever grateful.

'You'd better get busy teaching those assistants. I want you out and about as soon as possible, but you must see that the standards in here remain high.'

She stood up and stretched. 'I'll leave you to it.'

On Thursday morning the brilliant chandelier which has been recently hung in the centre of the ballroom at Worcester Guildhall, fell to the ground and was, of course, completely destroyed.

The card and dancing assembly was held the same evening and it is certainly a very fortunate circumstance that the accident did not happen at that time as the consequences would then, in all probability, have been very serious.

(Copyright and courtesy of the Worcester News)

CHAPTER THIRTEEN

'A star gazing tower?' Ruby repeated, looked puzzled.

Barnabus had become used to reporting to her and his confidence in proposing new ideas grew daily. He'd quickly learned to think a thing through thoroughly before presenting it and she'd become better at listening and debating, rather than issuing a flat no.

He'd demonstrated that he knew how to entertain a crowd and had proved more than capable of managing the staff and dealing with the most awkward customers in a discreet but firm manner. Thus far, she was impressed with the way he'd fitted into his new role.

'Tell me more.'

'What started me off was a conversation I overheard a couple of weeks ago. A chap was buying drinks and urging his friends to help him celebrate his new position. It turns out he's been taken on to guard a church tower from the folks who sneak in at night to map the stars.

'I dug around a bit and found out that people are constantly trying to get in to churches at night to scale the spires. It's a real problem that the churches want stamped out, but folk are turning up in droves to see what the fuss is about.'

She was bemused. 'I know they use the stars for navigation at sea but, do people really do it for fun?'

'It wouldn't entertain me. Lying on my back in the bitter cold and looking up at nothing was what I did night after night as a boy. Damned if I'll do it as a man.'

She shuddered in sympathy, familiar with his story.

'But this isn't about me.' He continued. 'Studying the stars has become fashionable and I think we should get in on it. Give them what a church spire offers, and more. A sturdy, tall structure with a large area to accommodate groups.

'The churches don't have space you see. If a fellow is up there, there's no room for others and that's what caused the problem. Some fool complained to the minister's wife, suggesting they should be made to take a turn each. They hadn't realised it was happening until then and that's put a stop to it.

'If we built something safe and roomy they'd pay to use it. I'm sure they would. What do you think?'

'I think they might.'

She laughed at the surprise on his face.

'You agree?'

'Mmhm. We need something new so it's worth considering. It would be no good at Sansome Springs, but there's always Sidbury. I'd certainly like you to gather up more information, talk to people and try to measure the interest, and I'll see what I can learn too.'

'Right.' He'd expected to have to argue his case and was nonplussed at her enthusiasm.

'Whole families could come to see the stars together. Tutors could bring their students.'

Her eyes sparkled with excitement. 'I can see the potential though I know nothing about the study of the stars. Do you?' She asked him.

He shook his head. 'No, but I'll learn.'

They sketched out a rough working plan and spent the next few weeks talking to people and reading everything they could find on the mystery of the skies.

Ruby then arranged to meet Francis - the man who'd made her dreams of a pleasure garden a reality - at the newspaper office. She trusted him absolutely and would do nothing without his advice.

'I think we could begin by installing a brick works here then we could have men firing bricks right away.'

As she described her vision of the tower her voice grew excited and her arms darted about, pointing out this and that.

'You're as energetic as ever.' Francis laughed as he scribbled notes. 'I can't think how we keep up with you.'

She laughed with him. 'Not everyone does but I know you of old, you'll be adding ideas in no time. I'll bet you have some thoughts already. Don't you?'

He nodded. 'One point?' He said and then waited for her nod.

'There's no reason to fire your own bricks. There are any number of brickworks that could supply us and deliver via the canal. I realise you want to offer work right away and we can still do that. We'll need extensive ground clearing here, levelling and digging out footings and that should be done as soon as possible. We can have good bricks delivered cheaply in no time.'

She nodded happily. 'So, if we go forward, you'd manage the project for me?'

'I'd be proud to.'

They shook hands. 'So long as you employ local men I'll leave all other decisions to you.' He nodded his agreement.

They continued to pace together, both putting forward ideas until it became too dark to see what they were doing. They parted company with Francis promising to put a proposal together and get back to her in a few days.

'I'm in hurry though, remember!' She called to him with a wave.

He answered with a wave. 'I'll proceed with haste, never fear.'

Now she'd decided to go ahead, there was no reason to delay, people came to her to be entertained and this would be a continuation of that, something new for them to marvel at.

That her new entertainment was to be situated at the opposite end of the city was a good thing. The more she thought about it the more convinced she became that schools and teachers would bring pupils to a place from which they could safely study the stars. Those people were highly unlikely to visit the pleasure gardens to do so.

The tower would be built on the highest point of her land, making it visible for miles, ensuring that every vehicle travelling to or from London would see it and be intrigued, whether they had an interest in the stars or not.

Ruby and Francis fell comfortably into their familiar custom of spending an hour each morning together, discussing the work as they monitored the digging out of the footings.

The men were thankful for the work and enjoyed the ale that was pressed on them in the inns at night by those who wanted to know exactly what it was they were building.

To a man they drank the beer and bragged about the star gazing tower, making up what they didn't know. They sang Ruby's praises as others shook their heads over her latest madness.

Persons willing to contract with the Trustees for making a New Road from the new Worcester Bridge to join the Turnpike Road in the Town of St Johns, according to Mr Gwynn's Plan, are desired to deliver their Proposals in writing, sealed up, to Mr Michael Brown, Clerk to the Trustees before Friday next. Estimates are desired for making and completing the road by the yard running measure.

(Copyright and courtesy of the Worcester News)

CHAPTER FOURTEEN

The new year blasted in on a tide of icy wind and slashing rain. Misery piled on misery as working outdoors proved impossible. In the city, people fared better than their country cousins, one small fire in a kitchen could warm up to twenty, if they didn't mind the huddle. No-one ventured far from home, the roads were a death trap, why risk it?

Ruby sat in her parlour, drumming her fingers on the table and driving herself mad, fretting about things she had no control over.

No-one was visiting her gardens, they were a frozen wasteland and the wind on the higher ground could cut a body in two. Work had stopped on the star gazing tower, the ground being too hard to dig. Ellie still wouldn't tell her what was wrong, and she was stuck in here watching Mary scan the newspaper.

'So, it says here that we're to be paying for a new gaol.'

'Hmmm.'

Mary laughed. 'Apparently half-a-dozen prisoners escaped when Nelson was here and never been seen since.'

'Hmmm.'

'It's easier to walk out of the gaol than it is to get out of Pargeters without buying something.

'It's a bit of a smack in the face though, expecting poor folk to dig deep to keep rogues locked up, and in the next breath they tell us how marvellous those rich bastards at the Porcelain are doing.'

'Hmmm'

'Rain's stopped.'

'Hmmm.'

'You're such good company. Always a smile and a cheery word.' Mary said as she ripped the paper to shreds and threw it on the floor.

'What?' Ruby frowned.

'I said you're a miserable, ungrateful cow and if you don't stop scowling the milk will sour. Fuck me Ruby, it's the dead of winter, what do you expect the weather to be like?'

'Sorry, I've got a lot on my mind.'

Mary rested her arms on the table. 'Tell me?'

'You always say you don't care about business.'

'I don't, not one bit. But God help us if you don't start talking soon we shall all go mad. I can ignore you running around being important and telling us all the odds, but this, looking like thunder and saying nothing, you're giving me the willies. Tell me what's on your mind?'

'I hear the river's frozen hard.'

Mary scratched her head and pulled her shawl closer. 'Makes me shiver thinking about it but it's solid. Jim Carter towed a wagon load of wood over the downriver of the bridge, he said it was worth risking his life to cheat Daventor of his toll. Gave him an extra hour to sup ale in the Talbot into the bargain.'

'Yes, that's what I thought.'

'Isaac Monter reckons to drive a herd of cattle over today, so a fellow from the Shambles tells me. They say it'll take weeks to thaw.'

'We should have an ice fair. A bit of food, nothing fancy, and some music, make something of it.'

72

Mary threw a log on the fire and cursed under her breath. *Me and my bleeding big mouth.* 'Who do you suppose is going to turn out to eat a slice of mutton in weather like this? Go back to brooding, I've got work to do.'

'Did you say the rain had stopped?' Ruby looked up with a grin.

'Don't miss a trick, do you? It stopped raining last night.'

Mary's warnings fell on deaf ears as Ruby wrapped herself in every cloak and shawl she could lay her hands on, determined to go out and see if she couldn't generate some interest in an ice fair.

The air was so cold that it hurt to do more than pant, but the sky was a clear, pale blue and the wind had stilled. She called on every tradesman between home and the pleasure gardens.

'You're doing no business, why not join in? We'll each take a stretch and put on our own food or music. Everyone will come, you'll see.'

Those that refused were given a pitying smile and promptly forgotten.

'When's it to be?'

'Tomorrow, we're all standing idle through this freeze and there's no threat of rain. It'll do us all good.'

Those that agreed would never forget the brilliant smile that warmed them.

By eight next morning a dozen crackling braziers lined the river bank from the Dog and Duck all the way out to the cathedral. The smell of cooking scented the air. Most of the innkeepers she'd approached joined in.

What she'd said was right enough, there was no trade calling in so why not go out and get it?

Bystanders huddled in knots around the heat while daring each other to skate out further and still further. Before long races from one side to the other were deemed unworthy and abandoned in favour of flying up and down, from the cathedral to the bridge, then on to the racing ground, then further still. The more they skated, the warmer they got, and the safer they felt.

Juliet Rhodes - who'd been on the stage before she'd caused a scandal by snaring the preacher and turning godly - took one step onto the ice and became that dancing girl again. One by one other women stepped out and soon a dozen or more were imitating her moves as she spun and twirled across the ice.

'Look at Reverend Rhodes all lit up and drooling over his own wife, there'll be another baby on the way by morning, you see if I'm wrong.'

'Bit of respect for the man of the cloth, Bella.'

'If you knew what I know you wouldn't waste your respect on him, dirty old devil.'

For the first time in her life milkmaid Betsy Taylor was a featherweight, and how she loved it, as did the men watching her. She was a picture of grace as she glided up and down, laughing for the joy of it, skirts flying and cheeks glowing.

The doomsters on the bridge who warned that the ice was cracking were silenced by Jeb Plum and his brother who hauled their cousin's massive printing press out to the centre of the Severn, the point they declared to be the weakest.

The massive press sat there, as solid as could be as they printed out a document, a copy of which was handed to anyone who dared walk, run, skate or even dance out to them.

One side of the document read,

The art of printing was invented by Lawrence John Koster and brought to England by Caxton and Turner in 1468.

And on the reverse,

His hoary frost, his fleecy snow
Descend and clothe the ground;
The liquid streams forbear to flow,
In Icy fetters bound.

The frost has been so particularly severe for the last fortnight that almost every part of the River Severn is frozen over so as to bear the weight of persons walking on it and crossing it. On Wednesday, several people going to Tewkesbury Market rode on horse back across the river.

All persons who are liable to be injured or incommoded by the overflowing of the Severn and other rivers would do well to prepare for a very high flood on the breaking up of the present ice and frost. The whole face of the country has been frozen several inches thick and should the thaw be sudden and accompanied with much rain a tremendous inundation may be expected.

(Copyright and courtesy of the Worcester News)

CHAPTER FIFTEEN

Ellie sat with her sewing basket and her lap and watched as Harold drew out the process of reading his newspaper, it was all she could do to hold back a scream. She was sick with nerves and her palms were too damp to wield a needle safely. She tried to maintain the illusion as he hated to see her idle.

He grunted, folded the paper neatly and placed it on the table at his side. 'Your notorious sister goes from strength to strength, I see.' He tapped the paper as he spoke, knowing she had no idea what he meant.

Normally this teasing might have upset her, but she was too full of her own news and the fear of telling him, to be diverted. She braced herself. 'Indeed, as do I.'

'Ha.' He started in surprise, she rarely said more than yes or no. 'Really?'

'Yes, I find I'm with child.' She spoke quickly, uncertain of his reaction but unable to conceal her own delight.

He stared at her blankly until she felt sweat prickle at the back of her neck. She bent to place her sewing on the floor, her hands shaking so badly, she upset the basket.

Harold walked across the room and leaned on the mantel. 'Are you quite sure?' He demanded.

She smiled and nodded. 'A baby, we're having a baby. I thought... I didn't think it would happen, my age...'

'Good God, neither did I. Well. That's ah, something to ponder.'

He left the room and she leaned back, closing her eyes, thankful he'd gone and wondering what there was for him to ponder. She was having a child and the only question in her mind was *does the news please him or not?*

She was thrilled and relieved. Her early symptoms had made her think she must be ill, she lost weight and was constantly tired. It was only after she'd been forced to withdraw from a consultation with an important customer to run to the closet, that Hannah pointed out the obvious to her.

Hannah, who had been beside her for twenty years, celebrated her joy as sincerely as she'd grieved for her past heartache. Clearly Ellie and her new husband had settled down and their marriage was safely on track.

On Monday, a female, the wife of John Radcliffe of Rodmarton, Gloucestershire and the mother of eleven children, with a halter around her neck, was exhibited for sale at Cirencester Market. She was received as a bargain by a young man for two shillings
(Copyright and courtesy of the Worcester News)

CHAPTER SIXTEEN

Harold didn't care one way or the other about having another child - three was not much different to two - but the testament to his own virility was naturally pleasing. His friends had dished out dire warnings about marrying an older woman and he'd enjoy parading her condition before them.

He regretted marrying her though. She took care of his sons and that was a blessing but how he wished he'd settled for paying a woman to do that, rather than marrying one.

His first wife had been a childhood friend and they'd shared a bond of love and trust that made their unconventional union a happy convenience for them both. In losing Clara though, he found he'd lost his desire to conform and was taking risks on an almost daily basis to find release.

The news of the pregnancy seemed to have calmed him, although he stayed away from home more frequently and for longer periods. She imagined he was getting used to the idea of another child and hoped his disappointment in her would be lessened if she gave him another son.

She took advantage of his gentler mood and mentioned that she would enjoy visiting Ruby.

He scowled. 'Yes, I suppose you'll want the support of your sister at a time like this.'

She thanked him and sent a message to Ruby, saying she'd call on her the following day. He was a complicated man but, with a baby on the way and his blessing to see her sister, she'd cope with his quirks and do her best to make him happy. All would be well.

She could barely get up from her bed the following morning, putting her feet on the floor had her doubled over with nausea. She sent a message to Ruby delaying her visit for a week and lay back down to sleep.

An hour later the hammering on the fancy black door knocker shook the house and had the maid fearing for her life as she opened it.

Ruby marched in and demanded to be taken to see her sister. The maid gaped and nodded before scuttling away leaving Ruby to cool her heels in a small room by the main door. She scanned her surroundings and saw that her sister's new home was very well appointed. Judging by the glow of the furniture, the fine drapery and glittering trinkets on display Ellie had moved up in the world.

Was this what had caused her to pull away, was Ellie ashamed of her? She'd always had finer tastes than Ruby and made no secret of her disdain for Ma and her work. Well, if her sister wanted to forget her humble roots, Ruby wouldn't stand in her way.

Ellie opened the door and carefully made her way across the room. She sat down with a sigh and smiled wanly at her sister.

'Oh lord, whatever ails you?' Ruby said, jumping to her feet as Ellie sat. She knelt before her sister and held her hands. 'What is it Ellie?'

'A sickness that hits me daily and lasts for hours.' Ellie said, placing her hands protectively on her stomach and smiling brightly.

'You're having a baby!' Ruby gasped in surprise. 'Why didn't I think of that?'

'For the same reason I didn't, I've left it a bit late.' Ellie cried.

The sisters embraced, holding on tightly for a long time. 'I'd given up hope of a family of my own years ago. I can barely believe how lucky I am. I don't care about the sickness or anything else. I'm having a baby Ruby.'

'I've been so worried about you.'

Ellie nodded. 'I know and I'm sorry. We had a difficult start, and we've both had to make allowances and take the time to get to know one another, but we're both happy about the baby and I'm sure things will improve. And his boys are a joy to be with, I love them both dearly and they love me back.'

The note of surprise in her voice touched Ruby. 'Oh Ellie, why wouldn't they love you?'

Ellie smiled and tried to be bright as she could, but nothing could disguise the dark circles below her eyes or the grooves that ran down either side of her mouth.

A late in life pregnancy was generally feared and Ruby reached over to give her sister a reassuring hug. The unexpected movement caused the sleeve of Ellie's dress to ride up exposing a livid yellow bruise encircling her thin wrist.

Ruby raised her eyebrows. 'What happened?' She asked, her voice flat.

Ellie pulled the sleeve down hastily. 'It's nothing, I stumbled, and Harold caught me. The bruise is yellow because it's old. It was weeks ago.'

She twisted her wrist this way and that, as though to demonstrate the damage was only on the surface. 'See, no lasting harm done and no need for you to make a fuss.'

Ruby's fears about Ellie's welfare came rushing back. 'I'm not making a fuss. You're hurt, and I'm concerned. You're as nervous as a cat so why not tell me what you're afraid of?'

Ellie turned deathly white as she heard Harold walking up the stairs. 'Please don't say anything to upset him. I promise you there's nothing I can't manage. I don't want the rift between you and him to go on. I need you in my life. Please!'

Ruby snorted her disgust but nodded as Harold opened the door.

He came first to kiss his wife's cheek and then welcomed Ruby to his home. His manners were courteous but did nothing to disguise a coldness that made the hairs on her neck stand on end.

She tamped down her revulsion and drank tea and made small talk for a polite fifteen minutes before excusing herself. Reluctant to do or say more until she knew what was really going on.

As she stood to leave, she felt the tension in the room ease. The couple were relieved that she was going and so, after urging her sister to retire to bed, she left them alone together.

Harold stood quietly beside his wife and watched her walk away. 'She's worn you out so why don't you do as she suggested and go to bed now. I'll have some food sent up for you?'

Ellie nodded weakly. 'I'm very tired but seeing her has lifted my spirits enormously. I'll do as you say and rest, but no food, please.'

He nodded his head. 'I'm happy to hear it. Now, to bed with you!'

She sank into her bed gratefully and slept deeply for hours.

When she woke she saw a drink by her bedside and drank it down thirstily before sliding back into sleep.

Ombersley Court, the seat of the Marchioness of Downshire, is undergoing considerable alterations. A new wing is now being added to the north end and the whole house is about to be cased in stone. It seems doubtful whether the Prince of Wales will visit the marchioness this year.
(Copyright and courtesy of the Worcester News)

CHAPTER SEVENTEEN

Progress on the construction of the star gazing tower was once again delayed but this time the mild weather was to blame. The footings that had been excavated and then frozen hard were now waterlogged and crumbling, working before the ground had a chance to dry out would endanger lives.

But Ruby couldn't keep away. An overdue visit to Richard and Elizabeth would answer several needs. She could discover what he was up to, talk to Jacob and John, listen to Elizabeth's latest gripe and survey her works at the same time. And of course, see her grandchildren.

The worksite was a quagmire and she felt disheartened, finding it impossible to tell what had been carved up by man and what by nature. She couldn't navigate a path over the ground without losing her balance. She realised it would be weeks before any progress could be made.

She turned away in irritation, she'd visit Richard and the girls, then have an hour in the newspaper office before returning home.

Richard swung the door open, he'd seen her at the brow of the hill, too far away to be recognised but who else would be mad enough to trudge around the mud up there?

'We weren't expecting you, were we?'

'No, but I wanted to see you and I thought it would be a good idea to listen to Elizabeth's objections in person.' She looked back at the path she'd followed.

'It's not the view she's upset about, you can't see anything from here, can you?'

He stepped back to let her pass. 'Come in.'

She breezed past the parlour door and on through to the kitchen, knowing that would infuriate Elizabeth who would never allow a visitor to set foot in there. She took a seat by the window and glanced across the courtyard towards the newspaper office and the little cottage that Ann and Sam had poured all their energy and love into, but that had never satisfied her daughter in law.

'It's not just Elizabeth.' Richard said.
'We're both worried about crowds being drawn to the area. The children are perfectly safe running about the grounds at will and we'd hate that to change. And we certainly don't want the type of noise and mess that surround Sansome Springs.'

Ruby snorted in disbelief. 'You're on the main route to London with traffic rolling by night and day, that causes far more disruption than my gardens do. The truth is Elizabeth resents living here and my new building has given her another reason to complain. She won't stop, she wants you to purchase one of the smart new houses being constructed in The Foregate. You know that as well as I.'

'My wife wants the best for our children and I support her.'

'You support her wishes, but financially, I support her. Your expenses rise year on year and my income must keep pace. You live very well out here, with your smart home and ridiculous carriage, not to mention four children. Does she have any idea how much all of that costs?'

'Ruby please.' He glanced nervously at the doorway.

She shook her finger at him and watched his lips purse. 'You're a fool if you're keeping secrets from her. I won't betray you, but are you being entirely fair?'

He clenched his fists and turned away. 'She wants so much, for us, for the children, I can't keep up with it all.'

Footsteps in the passage outside alerted them to Elizabeth's presence. 'What on earth are you doing in here? Ruby, how lovely of you to surprise us, won't you come through and see the children?'

Ruby smiled widely. 'I'd love too.'

Elizabeth led the way to the parlour and Ruby's heart lifted at the sight of the girls struggling to hold onto a part of the wriggling tyrant that was their baby brother, Thomas. They whooped with delight to see her.

She sat down and cuddled Thomas onto her lap as she replied to a flurry of questions from the girls. What was she building? When would the men come back? Would it be finished soon?

She told them about the star gazing tower. 'If you work hard at your lessons, I'll let you be the first people to go up if you like.'

Elizabeth sucked in her breath. 'I think that's quite enough now. Eliza, take Thomas to the playroom, and you two go with her, I'll be along in moments.'

Elizabeth waited until they'd gone before turning on Ruby. 'I'm opposed to your tower and I'll thank you to respect me on this. I can't prevent you from building it, but *my* children will have nothing to do with it.'

She cast a bitter glance at her husband, and left mother and son alone together.

Richard looked at Ruby in despair. 'I think you should go now.'

'Of course.'

To stonemasons: Wanted immediately, a number of masons that can work in hard and soft stone, where good wages and constant employ may be had by applying to William Stephens and Co, Worcester.
(Copyright and courtesy of the Worcester News)

CHAPTER EIGHTEEN

Ellie groaned, too sick to raise her head. She was home alone, Hannah was doing the work of two next door, and Harold was downstairs in his shop.

Not that she'd call on him for help. His violent outbursts had stopped and his behaviour towards her in public was solicitous, but at home he was remote, cold even, and she shrank from him.

He said all the right things and urged her to rest and not worry. He constantly produced drinks and potions to ease her symptoms, but lately, she'd feared his medicines were making her worse, and had decided to stop taking them.

She leaned on the dresser and waited for the usual dizziness to drift away and then she slowly made her way to the window, clinging to the sill for a moment to steady herself before reaching up to unfasten the catch.

Leaning out as far as possible, she gulped in cold, clean air. Icy raindrops splashed heavily onto the back of her neck and soaked her hair and she sighed with relief.

She'd never imagined she'd welcome such vile weather but since suffering the persistent headaches that had become a constant feature of her life, she'd learned that the only relief came from cold water trickling on her head and neck.

She folded her hands protectively over her stomach and prayed, for her own life and that of her child, more afraid than she'd ever been.

On Friday an Inquest was held on the body of Judith Beale, aged 17, who died by poison the preceding Wednesday. James Foster had paid his addresses to this young lady for some time and had brought her three pennyworth of mercury and had persuaded her to take a fourth of it, saying it would do her very little hurt and that he had known three or four who had taken it to procure an abortion. On the 21st she miscarried then died.

(Copyright and courtesy of the Worcester News)

CHAPTER NINETEEN

Elizabeth gripped the back of the chair, her face twisted in rage. 'Have you lost your mind?' She screeched. 'What about the children? Do you want them to be orphaned? And me, what is to become me?'

'Don't be ridiculous, I'm not abandoning you, I'm going to sign up. The French are expected to invade and this time I'm going to play my part.'

She laughed bitterly. 'You can't stand up to your own mother, never mind the French! What on earth do you think you can do for your country? You're deluded, and dangerous. You'll reduce us to the poorhouse.'

He sighed in exasperation. 'There's no question of the poorhouse. Joseph and John will keep the newspaper going with Ann overseeing them. They do most of the work now in truth.'

She looked for something to throw. 'Ann is at least sixty years old and crippled up with some disgusting ailment. Whatever you think you can, or cannot do, let me assure you Ann is not up to running your ghastly gossip sheet and I certainly won't be getting involved in the filthy business.' With that she burst into tears and ran from the room.

Richard grunted quietly and poured himself a drink. It hadn't gone too badly considering it was the first time he'd broached the subject, in fact, it was the first time he'd ever stood up to her. He looked in the mirror and raised the glass to himself.

He'd need to tell Ruby next and she'd fight him too, but at least she wouldn't crumble into hysterics. He'd go and get it over with today, but the weather was beyond foul and anyway, two battles in one day was asking too much. Tomorrow would be time enough.

But the morning brought heavy skies and a wind that whipped at everything standing and he decided to delay a visit to Ruby for another day.

Elizabeth continued to rage. 'You do not need to enlist! I read your stupid newspaper every day and I know men are going off to train for battle, but they have no choice, you do. Can't you be a man for once and say what's really in your mind.'

He bowed his head and ran his hands across his face. 'I'm sorry Elizabeth, my mind is made up.'

She stalked away from him in disgust. He'd always been weak and pathetic, but it had taken her years to see it. She couldn't bear to look at his stupid face. Planning to leave her here alone with their children while he rode off to get himself killed, the man was a lunatic.

She pressed her ear against the door to the children's room listening to their laughter until she felt her anger leave her, at another giggle from Thomas she smiled, her mood had lifted.

If there was a glue in their marriage Thomas was it. They were united in their love for him and shared a determination to ensure he grew up surrounded by happiness. This was what mattered, this was why she must be kinder to Richard. He couldn't be allowed to leave them, she had to make him stay.

She joined the children, seeing at once that Eliza, the princess, had organised a royal pageant and was parading through the village accompanied by two ponies - the twins – prancing and neighing at her sides.

She'd instructed Thomas to walk behind her as her page, but he, unaware of the rules and badly wanting to be a pony, insisted on prancing along.

Elizabeth executed a perfect curtsey and joined the royal pageant for a moment or two before gently trying to calm them all down. They fell into a collapsed heap on the rug begging her to read them a story before lunch.

After lunch they'd have lessons with Ann and she and Thomas would nap, a routine that had begun when the twins arrived.

Eliza had been a spoilt toddler until then, used to having her parents undivided attention and unprepared to share. She was confused at being expected to take a back seat to the twins and threw tantrums if she saw Elizabeth nurse them. Richard was treated to storms of tears daily.

Ann was their salvation, stepping in to make Eliza her own special project, giving Elizabeth time with the twins. Calm was restored and although Elizabeth and Ann would never be friends, they developed a mutual respect that carried the day.

As the twins grew from babies into girls they were permitted to sit with Eliza for lessons. Ann cherished the girls and was good for them. She was calm and even-handed and was a stickler for routine.

By the time Thomas arrived the practice was firmly established, allowing Elizabeth to devote all her time to this precious little boy.

Today, like every other day, Ann left the cottage she shared with Ben and walked across the courtyard to the family house.

Hearing the door open, Elizabeth turned to greet her. 'There you are Ann, bless you for coming over in this weather, come closer to the fire and get warm.'

Ann stretched her chilled fingers toward the blaze. 'It's no distance and the wind's dropped a treat. It'll be all over in no time.'

'Well, we're grateful you came, aren't we girls?' Elizabeth spoke in a jolly tone and was instantly furious with herself. Why could she not be comfortable around this woman? The entire family were devoted to her, yet she was reduced to idiocy in her presence.

'How's Ben, I haven't seen him for a day or two?'

'He's worried about his plants of course, we've had a few small fruit trees ripped up which grieves him. But he's well enough.' Ann shrugged. 'He'll be out there working later, no doubt.'

Elizabeth nodded, she'd been warm and civil and now she could leave. 'I think I'll take Thomas out for a breath of air. We've been housebound for days.'

'Oh, I really ...'

'Just a few steps across the courtyard, as you said, it's no distance. We'll be curled up together in the parlour beside the fire before your lessons have begun. Be good for Ann, girls!'

Ann began the routine that she'd established many years before when she and Sam had taken Richard into their home and their hearts. What had helped him then was helping his girls now, a moderate dose of book teaching and large dose of explanation and humour was Ann's way to keep pupils engaged.

She tested them on yesterday's lesson and then told them what she wanted from them today and they sat quietly scribbling away as she strolled down memory lane.

She was startled awake by a banging door, the stiffness in her neck telling her she'd been asleep for a while. She eased out her shoulders and threw a log on the fire as Richard strode into the room.

'Still here Ann? You should be tucked up at home now. Come along, I'll see you across the courtyard.'

'There's no need for that.' She protested guiltily, she must have slept for an hour, if not longer.

He bent and kissed her cheek. 'Every need for it, I've not seen you for days and you've surely missed me!' They laughed companionably as he held out her cloak.

'Eliza, run and fetch Mama. It's time we all ate.' He spun around with a growl. 'And you two can tidy away your books.' The twins giggled up at him.

Ann kissed their shining faces as they chorused their goodbyes, Richard put his arm around her to escort her home.

It was thirty minutes or so later that he returned to the house to find Eliza anxiously waiting for him. 'I can't find Mama, she's not anywhere. I've called and called her.'

In the background he heard the familiar sounds of the twins fighting and he winked at her. 'How about this, you try to stop your sisters killing each other and I'll go and find Mama? I expect she's cuddled up warm with Thomas somewhere.'

He dropped a kiss on her forehead and watched her scamper away, happy to be officially charged with ordering the twins about.

'Elizabeth.' He called as he ran up to the second floor. 'Where are you?' His voice quieter now and somewhat puzzled. He went from room to room and, finding no sign of her or their son, ran back down to check each room on the ground floor. They were nowhere to be found.

He heard the clatter as the maid laid out their meal. 'Peters, a word please.' He indicated with his head that she should step into the hall. 'When did you last see my wife?'

'I haven't seen her today Sir. I had this morning off as my mother is sick and needed my help at home. I returned an hour or so ago and went directly to prepare tea for the girls.'

He ran his fingers through his hair in distraction. 'Very well.'

He went back across the courtyard to Ann's, hammering on the door before letting himself in, calling out a hello as he did so.

Both Ben and Ann came running, 'I can't find Elizabeth and Thomas, did she go out? It's not like her to be away at tea time.'

'She said Thomas needed some air.'

Richard backed away, muttering that he must find her, and Ben quickly followed him outside. Ann draped herself with an old coat that covered her from head to toe and, after arming herself with a sturdy stick, slammed the cottage door shut.

Joseph and John came out to join the search and, as soon as the torches were lit, the small search party headed to the open side of the courtyard and the small-holding that Ben managed, beyond that lay Ruby's new project.

It was an hour later that Joseph saw Elizabeth trapped under a fallen tree, her body curled around baby Thomas. The gouges in the mud and the blood on her arms told how desperately she'd fought for their lives.

Peters watched from the house as they returned. Ben and Joseph carried the body of Elizabeth and Richard followed with Thomas while Ann and John held the torches aloft to light their way.

Hearing the twins upstairs, teasing and giggling Peters shouted up to them. 'Come down here now.'

For the first time ever, they obeyed her, still giggling but unsettled by her tone. Eliza followed them down, her eyes lowered and her face pale. Peters drew them into the kitchen.

Hoofs clattered across the stones and men's voices were a rumble that ebbed and flowed, words unclear but mood distinct. A door slammed, and footsteps headed to their door.

Ann came in first, with Richard close behind. The girls ran to their father looking for reassurances he was unable to give. They listened, wide eyed, as he told them that their Mama and precious little Thomas were gone. The twins folded into each other in tears as Eliza leaned into Richard and buried her sobs.

He scooped the three of them onto his chest and held them as they cried.

Ann pulled Peters from the room. 'He won't want to eat, but he'll need to and it's up to us to make it as easy as we can for all of them.'

Peters nodded doubtfully. She'd only come back today to tell Elizabeth she had to return home as her father needed her. This family's tragedy on top of her own was too much to bear. She was barely able to do more than listen and obey Ann's instructions.

She couldn't leave them tonight of course but, hard as it would be, tomorrow she was going home to nurse her mother. She tried to tell Ann, but that poor woman was only just holding herself together.

Ruby would be with them soon, they just had to hold on until then, they might be out of their depth, but Ruby, well, she could cope with anything!

In consequence of the sudden and rapid thaw of snow and ice, almost every river in the kingdom has overflowed its banks, and immense tracts of land have been laid under water. The Severn rose to a height which has not been witnessed for many years and is only 18 inches below the plate which was placed at the Worcester cathedral Watergate to commemorate the great flood of 1770.

(Copyright and courtesy of the Worcester News)

CHAPTER TWENTY

Ruby effectively became the head of the household.

Richard had almost lost his mind and rejected his daughters, becoming surly and aggressive when they turned to him for comfort.

'They're your damn grandchildren, you do something with them.' He screamed at Ruby's suggestion that he might want to spend some time with them. He'd stormed out and returned two days later, dishevelled and stinking of stale ale.

Ann was a trembling wreck, convinced that she should have prevented Elizabeth going for a walk or at the very least raised the alarm earlier.

'For god's sake, no-one ever stopped Elizabeth from doing what she wanted, don't be ridiculous.' Ruby snapped.

'Richard's useless, Peters has gone home, and I need to be able to depend on you. How will the girls cope if they can't turn to you when I lose my temper? And you know I will.'

Ruby watched helplessly as her ordered and deeply satisfying life unravelled, one strand at a time. She regretted it, but these girls needed the stability and security that only she could offer. Everything safe had been torn from them and she had to steer them safely through.

But if she was to do that she'd need to delegate much of what she most enjoyed doing.

Lou, out at the nursing home, rarely asked for help. She was competent and content doing a job she loved, but still she had to be informed.

'Don't worry about us Ruby. I know what I'm doing out here. You take care of your family and I'll take care of these babies.'

Jacob and John were given the responsibility they'd craved for years. 'You'll work alongside Ann. I'll expect a monthly report from you, aside from that do your best to keep up the good work.'

Hannah was charged with keeping as close an eye on Ellie as possible and, in the event of anything untoward, was to send a message to Bella.

'Leave it to me Rube, one step out of line and I'll wring his miserable neck.' Bella appeared excited at the prospect.

Sansome Springs was the tough one, it was her pride and joy. She'd devoted everything to building them and nothing gave her more pleasure than walking the pathways and conjuring up new attractions. Relinquishing control was painful, but she saw no alternative.

Barnabus understood. 'I'll report to you every week and you'll know everything before I do it, I promise I won't let you down.'

She inclined her head. 'I'm fortunate to have you.'

She kept her envy of his freedom tamped down. Family came first but still …

After the funerals of Elizabeth and Thomas, she and Mary moved into the family home, preferring not to uproot the children. Mary was good for them, she had no time for tears or whining but was quick to laugh and admired a bit of spirit. No tears, but common sense and good food, these were her tools.

Ruby ordered work on the star gazing tower to cease. The very thought of it being built was abhorrent to her.

The secretary of State for the Home Department has fixed the rate of bounty for men to be raised by beat of drum for the Militia at four guineas.
(Copyright and courtesy of the Worcester News)

CHAPTER TWENTY-ONE

The dream of holding her own baby in her arms made a miserable pregnancy tolerable for Ellie. She'd stopped being sick every day and her appetite improved.

As her health improved she began to spend time each day with Hannah. She missed their friendship, and she felt out of touch with her business.

They slipped back into their old ways easily.

'You look better than ever Ellie.' Hannah said one day as they paused to take a break.

Ellie straightened up and stretched out her back. 'I feel on top of the world. It's staggering really, to go from feeling so ill to feeling this good.' She shook her head. 'I did wonder if I was being poisoned.'

'Oh God. Ellie, that's dreadful.' Hannah looked at her in horror. 'But, he'd be the first they looked at. You can't be right.'

'Well, perhaps not. I want you to promise me something though.'

Hannah looked up with a question in her eyes.

'Don't tell Ruby too much about what's going on here. I know she's been talking to you and I promise you I'll keep myself safe, but she has so much to cope with and I don't want her to be worrying about me. Will you promise me?'

Hannah nodded vigorously. She hated being involved in this awful business at all, but Ellie had been her confidante for many years and she wouldn't fail her.

'I won't say a word, so long as you promise to confide in Bella. That way I'll know that someone is on hand to help if we need them.'

Ellie reluctantly gave her agreement and they turned their conversation to more mundane matters regarding Madame Eloise.

Hannah had developed her own way of doing things during Ellie's absence and now she tried hard not to step on her toes. Neither was ready to acknowledge that with a new baby Ellie would not be returning to work. That was a problem for another day.

Bella visited Ellie once a week and both had dreaded it. Bella was too outspoken, verging on the rude and she'd die if the boys heard some of things she said.

Bella sneered at their smart house and elaborate furniture. She'd prance up the stairs behind the maid and try to engage the girl in conversation.

'Leave her alone Bella.'

'Just being friendly duchess.'

Bella despised Harold and her opinion of Ellie was little better, and she didn't trouble to hide the fact. She thought Ellie was reaping what she'd previously sowed, she'd always said Ellie was too big for her britches.

The two had first met years ago when Ellie found herself without work or a home. Ruby had taken her in, although it had been clear to everyone that Ellie was out of place.

Bella considered her stuck up and lazy, while Ellie only ever referred to Bella as *that woman*. The only thing Bella and Ellie had in common was respect for Ruby and so the weekly visits were something they both were prepared to endure.

They were both wrong footed to find that, after an uneasy start, they enjoyed these weekly encounters.

Bella was always at her best when she had an audience that she could shock with tales of her exploits, and she had a wealth of them to share. Ellie proved deliciously easy to tease, being alternately shocked and thrilled with the stories she heard.

Bella loved life and enjoyed men and was certain she could help Ellie straighten Harold out. She was biding her time and building Ellie's confidence before she embarked on her re-education.

Bella was easy to confide in, nothing shocked or horrified her and her ribald sense of humour and ability to find comedy in things that Ellie abhorred convinced her that though Harold's taste's might be specialised, they were by no means unique.

'I think he was poisoning me. That's why I was being so sick!'

Bella disagreed. 'Violent men don't generally take to poison, and I know he's thumped you in the past. Trust me, if he wanted you dead he'd have pushed you down the stairs or smothered you.'

Ellie shuddered as she recognised the truth in Bella's words.

'He was giving me something to make me sick, I know he was, so what was he after?'

'He wants you to be scared.'

'Why on earth would he want that?'

'Because he's weak as piss and wants the upper hand. That's it and all about it. He married you because he wanted Madame Eloise, and he thought you'd be useful looking after his brats. He's furious that he didn't get what he wanted, and he's stuck with you. Any pain you suffer is no more than you deserve in his tiny mind. It's up to you to put a stop to it.'

'I know why he married me, I admit I was fooled at first but that soon passed. I don't know how to make him treat me any better though?'

'He didn't do you any lasting damage and by the size of you I reckon the baby's unharmed so all we have to do is set him straight on a few things and you'll go along well enough.'

What had seemed like a tragedy to Ellie appeared to be all in a day's work to Bella. 'Life's so easy for you isn't it?'

Bella laughed richly. 'Life's good if you don't mind getting dirt on your hands. Men are simple creatures and as soon as you realize that and treat him right the happier you'll be.'

Ellie shook her head vehemently. 'I can't be like you Bella.'

'Well you got that right Duchess! You wouldn't find me putting up with the mess you're putting up with. I'd have battered that miserable streak of piss months ago.

'You need to stop pretending to be a lady and start acting more like your sister, and that I know you can do. The first thing is to put a bit of distance between the two of you for a few days.'

'I don't think Harold would permit that, he's very concerned about what people think.'

'Christ Ellie, we're talking about the fellow that'll give you a slap for the hell of it, the fellow that blacked your eye so's you couldn't work for two weeks. The fellow that kept you from your sister.'

Bella slipped her cloak back around her shoulders, not bothering to hide her disgust. 'If you're going to worry about what he approves of, I've been wasting my time. You're beyond help.'

'No. Don't go, you're right, he's everything you say, and I do need your help. I don't know how to manage him, and I'm going to have to learn. I can't continue in this way.'

Bella nodded. 'Fair enough. Say nothing tonight, keep things peaceful until we're ready to make our move.'

'What shall I do in the meantime? I need to be prepared.'

'No, you don't. You'll give the game away. You keep things as normal as you can and leave me to worry about details. What you don't know, you can't let slip, can you?'

Ellie nodded her head weakly and watched Bella leave. She carefully cleared away all trace of the the visit although Harold knew she was calling every week at Ruby's instigation.

He constantly muttered about all the bloody women checking his movements, but as he confined himself to cursing under his breath Ellie ignored him, choosing the path of discretion rather than valour.

A runaway-Hannah, a Parish apprentice to Mr Joseph Williams of Inkberrow, left her master's service two weeks ago and has not been since heard of. This is to forewarn all persons from harbouring the said girl or they will be prosecuted as the law directs. She is a short, fresh coloured young woman, about 16 years old, had on a brown coat, white straw hat with blue silk flowers round the crown, and carried a large bundle under arm. (Copyright and courtesy of the Worcester News)

CHAPTER TWENTY-TWO

Barnabus strolled around Sansome Springs savouring the feeling of being king of all he surveyed. It might be a temporary situation, but if he could improve on their constant struggle to attract a decent crowd in poor weather who knew how Ruby might view his future.

Drawing a crowd in the summer was easy, there was nowhere prettier to be. But now, surrounded by bare trees and shrubs and the fountains at a standstill the place offered little to tempt people from the comfort of home. It was a safe place for a walk if one longed for fresh air on a dry day, but in the rain or after dark it was different matter.

The casino was always packed, but they were there for the gaming and regardless of what else was on offer they'd be stuck in there, night and day. It generated a steady flow of revenue which more than covered its own costs, but both he and Ruby wanted more.

He shivered when he reached the old spring. When these gardens were first constructed a great hollow had been dug around the natural spring. It had been tiled and then allowed to fill with the spring water creating a natural bathing pool. Small groups of seats were dotted about with aromatic herbs planted between them.

This clearing had bothered Barnabus for some time. It should have been a light and airy spot but had been ill thought out and was dismal and dank.

Francis and Ben had created it for Ruby when she'd been mourning Tom. They meant well but they lacked her vison, the sad little spot had never been a success.

He sauntered on, churning the sad little spot over in his mind, oblivious to the cold. What would he do here if these gardens were his? He let his imagination soar, there were only dreams, after all.

Whenever he could find the time he visited nearby towns to see how other attractions coped with the winter months. Malvern and Cheltenham were as deserted as Worcester, confirming that he needed something neither of them had.

He talked to Ben and Francis, and then he consulted Dennis and Lillian Jones, all four had been beside Ruby from the start and he knew she trusted them all.

He had the germ of an idea but knew her well enough to know their approval would make a huge difference when he had to convince her. Within weeks he had people out and about, sketching, costing, and exploring the feasibility of his plan, each one sworn to secrecy.

By the time he had a request to visit Ruby in The Foregate house he had a plan ready and was delighted that he didn't have trek all the way out to Sidbury to present it.

Going out there was a constant reminder of the star gazing tower that would never be. He completely understood why it had to be stopped but, dammit, it could have been a wonderful thing.

He gathered everything he thought he needed and set off to Ruby's with a spring in his step.

'I've decided to move the girls here with me, I can't live out there, we're all missing out on too much.

They know nothing of Worcester and I plan to change that.'

Ruby rarely discussed her private life with him and he kept quiet, reluctant to break the spell.

'I think they'll do better here in town. There are too many reminders out there, and it's not healthy for them to be moping around in the family home every day. A change of scenery will be a distraction for them.'

Her stay at Richard's house had reminded her of her own childhood in St Johns where she'd learned that all manner of nastiness could be hidden behind neat cottages and tidy fields. It was easy to think nothing ugly happened in the country but that was as far from the truth as it was possible to get.

No one appreciated personal freedoms more than Ruby, but there was no denying having close neighbours encouraged better behaviour.

Her tipping point had come just days previously when she'd been manhandled by a crowd of men racing along in front of the church all full of ale and ready for the monthly bull baiting.

She'd been about ten years of age when she'd seen Hugh and William sneaking out to see a bull baiting. Ruby let them get on their way and then dragged a reluctant Ellie out to follow them, why should boys have all the fun?

William was furious when he caught them. 'They won't let girls watch, it's bad luck. You'll have to hide.'

The four of them scrambled up into a hayloft urging each other to be silent in between fits of giggles. It was exciting and fun as they organised themselves into a row, all lying flat on their bellies and able to peer down as the men assembled.

They watched jugs of ale being passed from hand to hand as the men inspected the snarling dogs that were tethered close enough to smell the bull. Some were solid brutes with huge heads and thick necks who snarled and dribbled as they were poked with sticks. Others danced about on spindle legs, nervously skittish. Some were little more than puppies whilst older, tougher looking beasts bore their battle scars proudly.

The men grew more boisterous, a fistfight started, causing a wave of cheers. The tall man hit the smaller fellow and a splash of blood shot out. Ruby felt sick as the man dropped like a stone to the floor.

She bitterly regretted joining this adventure but there was no escape, the hayloft was surrounded by the drunken men and they must stay here until the show was over.

A shout went up and the terrified bull was led into the circle and tethered. He was nervous, tossing his head about and snorting out great strings of snot. The men stepped back, and a couple of dogs were sent in.

It took the beast a while to realize the dogs were there to attack him, he appeared startled when the first one leapt up and took a bite, attaching himself to his face. With a howl of pain, the bull tossed his great head and the crowd cursed as the dog's neck snapped.

That carcass was kicked into the crowd, money changed hands and more dogs were sent in. The routine was repeated, the bull tossed his head with one dog attached and then again with three animals hanging off him.

The crack of a back or neck snapping was sickening as was the sight of a half-dead dog writhing on the ground and screaming out fear. The ones that had been bred for the purpose clung on unharmed, it was the others that provided sport for the men. Some dogs were wily enough to let go as the bull raised his head and they went in time and again, doing more damage to shambling beast with every bite.

His face was torn to shreds, his eyes were chewed, and his ears ripped, the snot ribbons were thick and red and the froth streaming from his mouth flew about and covered many of the men. The howls of the mortally wounded beast grew weaker as the men grew more raucous.

The four children in the hayloft lay petrified, their eyes closed and their hearts promising God that if he would let this end they would never disobey the rules again.

It was seeing the men that week that helped her decide to remove the girls from the countryside. Bull baiting was forbidden within city bounds and God knew she wouldn't wish any child to witness such barbarity.

'That's enough about us, to business, what are you up to out there?'

They spent an hour or so going over the reports that he'd prepared for her and there were few surprises.

'These numbers are no worse than usual at this time of the year.' She said in a matter of fact voice. 'But you've got something else on your mind and it's almost bursting out of you so spit it out.'

He cleared his throat. 'We're always worrying about how to increase our visitors during poor weather like this.'

She nodded for him to continue.

'I believe we need to build an area that is permanently under cover, somewhere that we can light a fire and those inside can be protected from the elements. I've had some drawings done to show you what I have in mind.' He handed her a roll of paper and held one end as she unrolled it.

She scanned it quickly, paused and looked over it again, minutely. 'It's made of glass?' She said.

He nodded. 'A glass and brick building that we can construct over the spring. We'd open it up in the daytime for ladies only. We'd serve tea, have music, they could play cards, meet with friends. They might bathe or drink the waters.'

She nodded thoughtfully. 'Who made these drawings?'

'Dennis Jones. I wanted to find similar structures that had already been built and that way get a better feel for what could be achieved. He was good enough to spend a couple of days with me.'

Ruby shuffled the papers once more before asking, 'Is Dennis the only friend of mine you've recruited?'

'No, I've talked at length with Lillian, Ben, Ann and Francis.'

She studied the sketches and he wiped the sweat from his brow. She'd gone along with his idea for a star gazing tower, but her recent tragedy might have killed her spirit of adventure.

'And what do my friends think of your idea?' Ruby asked.

'It's really a product of all our thoughts, I want to provide something that respectable ladies can take advantage of, and we have to do something big. Every year we worry about how long or cold the winter will be. But that's foolish, the winter is what it is. It's us that must change, surely. Don't you agree?'

'I do. Give me details.' She drummed her fingers on the table but kept her eyes on his drawings as he spoke.

'We'll construct supporting pillars all around the spring area and between each pillar will be glass doors, these will ensure light, air and easy access to the outside in summer. I want a grand fireplace, big enough to warm the whole space in poor weather. I imagine we'll place small tables dotted about with a variety of seating. This way ladies can be part of a group or sit in pairs or even singly if they choose.'

'Ladies?'

He nodded. 'Yes, a refuge for ladies is what I have in mind. No-one else has done that and I'm convinced they'll all come to sample it. I picture a raised platform here.' He stabbed at the drawing. 'For musicians and the like. And over here will be the fireplace. It will be comfortable and relaxing.'

'It all sounds wonderful, I can picture it perfectly, but the cost will be unimaginable!' She spoke kindly, she loved the vision he'd placed before her and she appreciated his sadness at the loss of the tower.

'Not so. You've already committed to the purchase of bricks for the tower. They're in the wrong place, but Mr Daventor will move...'

'You've spoken to Hugh about this?'

'Good Lord no!' He paled at the thought. 'Francis proposed that, I've never even met the man.'

Ruby nodded. 'Well, it's true enough, I've bought a huge amount of bricks that I thought Francis was attempting to return. Clearly he has other plans.'

He flushed but saw her smile. 'You like it don't you?'

'There's a lot to consider. I'll need to know where the glass will come from, and we must be clear about the costs and how long the whole thing will take to construct. The gardens must remain open throughout the building work so how will that arranged safely? Who will manage the work?

'You get those details answered, and draw up an outline of works and, if you convince me that you can manage all that and run the gardens we'll talk again. But you're right, I like it very much.'

He whistled softly as he walked back out of the city. The pleasure gardens were not his, but he loved them with all his heart just the same.

On Wednesday of last week, one of these disgraceful scenes was exhibited on Pitchcroft, and on Monday the same animal which was baited on the above day, was again brought forth to undergo a repetition of the cruelties it had before endured. We will not disgust our readers with a detail of the poor animal's sufferings nor display the dreadful spectacle which it exhibited. What courage is there in tying and animal to a stake and setting a number of dogs on it to savage it?
(Copyright and courtesy of the Worcester News)

CHAPTER TWENTY-THREE

Bella had discovered that Harold was in the habit of visiting a particularly disreputable inn on the outskirts of Droitwich once or twice a week. She timed her visit to coincide, confident he'd be away for the day and possibly through the night.

Despite there being little fear of his early return, she refused the offer of tea. 'No time for social nonsense today Duchess, I want you packed up and ready to go.'

'What? Where? What do you mean?'

'I asked you to trust me. Let's get away from here, then we can spend all the time you want chattering. If he should come back early, we'll miss our chance.'

Ellie shook her head stubbornly. 'I can't just pack up and go, I'm responsible for two small boys, and Madame Eloise. I can't just walk away.'

Bella looked at her in disgust. 'What do you think I am? The boys will be coming with us and Hannah's used to working without you, why don't you stop looking for excuses and start packing. I'll tell you the plan while we work, what do you say to that?'

Ellie sighed, but began to gather up essentials.

'The first thing is to get you three out of here. Lou had agreed to let you move into the nursing home. Once your clear, I'll come back and hide myself away until he came home, then once he's asleep, I'll whack him with the poker and then turn the shop upside down to make it look like a robbery.'

Ellie gasped and clapped her hand over her mouth. She sank onto the bed, her face a picture of horror. 'You must be mad. I could never go along with a scheme like that. Kill the father of those two little boys? Have you any idea what that would do to them, not to mention my unborn child? I won't listen to any more of your nonsense.'

Bella buried her face in her hands, shoulders shaking. 'Ruby said you wouldn't go along with it. She only let me come and tell you about it because she knew you wouldn't agree.'

'Do you have a sensible idea or am I to sort this mess out alone?' Ellie was bitterly disappointed, she'd foolishly thought Bella might be the one to rescue her and she felt badly let down.

Bella muttered to herself. 'I'd have killed the bastard months ago myself, but we're all different I suppose.'

'Bella!'

'You're such a prissy miss, I'm tempted to wallop you myself. I have got you a place with Lou and I do want you, and the boys to get packed up now. It'll be easier if we don't see him, but we'll be leaving him a letter telling him you've moved to the birthing hospital because you don't feel you can manage alone. He knows how sick you are, he can't object to that.'

'He'll be beside himself with fury.'

'He's got you too scared to think straight. He'll act up because he likes to give out the orders, but that's all top show to keep you down. He'll be glad to have you out of his hair with no chance of gossip.

'He wants his freedom, but he needs his reputation intact. You're not well and it's perfectly sensible for you to head out of the city to have your baby in a safe place. And who could criticise you for taking the two small boys you're mothering with you?'

A smile, faint but encouraging lightened Ellie's face. 'Yes.' She said thoughtfully.

'When he comes out to see you, as we know he will, you'll stop him in his tracks. You'll tell him you were in pain and found walking difficult and were worried about the boys, if you lost the baby. It's an obvious place thing for you to. There's a nurse on hand to take care of you, and the boys will have a handful of playmates to keep them happy.'

'He won't like it.'

'He won't like you thinking for yourself, but that's a problem for another day. Once you're there and safe, he'll have to deal with it. You're a good little wife, doing what's best for you and the baby.

'When you're settled, we'll talk about how you can put an end to his tricks when you come back. And you can, you just need to believe it. Are you with me, or not?'

'Yes. I'll get the boys.'

'Good girl, I'll get these boxes loaded onto the wagon.'

They left without a backward glance and were installed at the nursing home in a matter of hours. The boys were excited to be somewhere new and raced about whooping when they saw the open fields that were free to run and play in.

Lou introduced herself to Ellie. The skinny little girl with the limp who loved babies so much had grown up into a rosy cheeked, rotund woman, as broad as she was tall. She still limped but she was strong and full of love for her babies. She reassured Ellie that she'd made the right choice.

'I've delivered hundreds of babies so don't you worry about a thing, I'll take care of you, and you can stay as long as you need to.'

'You're very kind.'

Lou shook her head. 'I remember growing up at Ma's, Ruby was the one who made sure I was treated fair, told them all I was as good as anybody else.'

'I didn't know.'

'I have a wonderful life and Ruby made it possible. I'm proud to help her sister now.'

'I'm grateful. I hadn't realized that you'd been there, at Ma's I mean.'

'Oh, I was born there. Ma couldn't sell me on though, who'd want a girl with a withered leg? I was pretty much forgotten until Ruby came along. I can't tell you how much I owe her.'

Ellie nodded sleepily.

'Get some rest now, and don't worry about the boys, I'll let them have an hour or so of running wild and I'll find some jobs to wear them out.'

Ellie closed her eyes, exhausted after using all her courage to make her escape.

It was all well and good for Bella to say she must learn to manage Harold, but could she do that? She wasn't made of the same stuff as Bella and Harold knew it. Yet something had to change. She couldn't continue to live in fear and she certainly couldn't leave him.

She had to find a way to make the home a safe and happy place.

Until she found the answer, she'd remain in this spotless cottage and think of nothing but her baby.

It gives us real pleasure to find that the finances of the lying in charity, established in Worcester, are in so flourishing a state that during the last year no fewer than 253 poor women were relieved through its means during childbirth. We trust that the charity will still continue to receive that liberal support which its benevolent design so justly entitles it to.
(Copyright and courtesy of the Worcester News)

CHAPTER TWENTY-FOUR

The motherless twins turn away from the world and into each other, they slept entwined and held hands when they were awake. They whispered to one another but fell silent when anyone approached them, not even speaking to Eliza.

'They don't cry, they don't complain, they don't ask for anything. I don't know what to do for them.' Mary said, scraping out the dough she'd been mixing.

Ruby, on the other side of the table, put down her cloth. 'I think they're getting what they need from each other for now. It's Eliza that worries me. She seems to think the twins are her responsibility and it upsets her dreadfully to be ignored by them. The poor little thing is like a ghost drifting about and I'm damned if I know how to help her.'

Mary continued pounding at the bread dough as she considered Ruby's last comment. 'I should say you're doing enough by letting her stick close. She's scared to death to lose sight of you for fear you'll disappear along with the rest of them I reckon. She needs to trust that you're here to stay and you can thank Richard for planting that fear in her mind.'

'Mary.' The note of warning rang clear but was ignored.

'What? Am I still forbidden to utter a word about him? Turning his back when they need him most? Pah, he could be the difference those babies need if he would only put them first, but we both know he won't. Now, take your dirty looks out of my kitchen and see to your grandchildren while I get some food ready for us all.'

Ruby sat with the girls as they had their meal and then she prepared them for bed. They were listless but obedient and her heart was wrung out, nurturing was alien to her nature and she was at a loss. She longed to hear the peals of laughter and re-telling of adventures she'd come to expect but these sad little scraps were a world away from that.

Damn Richard and damn his spoilt selfish wife, between the two of them they'd blighted three young lives and she wouldn't find it easy to forgive him.

He stayed away for days on end paying no attention to his responsibilities and Ruby feared that if she couldn't wake him up, she'd be the one bringing these girls up. Once they were in bed she went back to sit with Mary.

'I'll have to find someone to help us.'

'Help you, you mean.' Mary sniffed.

'Someone young enough to show them how to have fun, be a pal to Eliza. I'll always be here but I don't know how to be a mother…'

'You'll learn as you go along if you want too, that's how it works.'

'You were right, what you said about Richard. Earlier.'

Mary nodded.

'I blame myself though, I was never a mother to him, so he doesn't know how to be a proper father.'

Mary stood up impatiently and began to clear the table. 'That's all in the past though my love. Maybe your mother was bad, maybe you could have done a better job, I couldn't say. But put it out of your head and think about them, make it right this time, no excuses.'

She placed the stacked dishes on the side table and make sure the fire was guarded before opening the door. 'I'm going to bed. Just remember this, it's not your fault Elizabeth and Thomas died, but it's not theirs either.' She pointed to the ceiling.

'If Richard won't take responsibility, you'll have to.'

On Sunday next two sermons will be preached at the Angel Street Meeting House, Worcester, to raise subscriptions for the benefit of the Sunday Schools attending there. From 110 to 150 poor children are taught to read on every Lord's Day at these schools, and the most deserving of them have the advantage of learning to write on weekday evenings.
(Copyright and courtesy of the Worcester News)

CHAPTER TWENTY-FIVE

Rapid footsteps drummed along the passage outside of her room giving Ellie seconds to brace herself. She smoothed down her hair and lifted her chin, then released a nervous laugh when Bella poked her head in.

'The bastard's here, shall I let him in or shall I kick his arse?'

Ellie grinned. Meeting Lou and having a peaceful sleep had done wonders. 'Let him in, but don't go too far away?' Bella winked and closed the door.

Harold stormed in. His anger was terrible, he pulled her letter from his pocket and waved it angrily in her face. 'What's the meaning of this nonsense Madam? I come home from work to learn that my entire family has gone away? Explain yourself.'

Ellie pressed her hands lightly on her swollen belly and inhaled deeply. 'Won't you sit down, I'd like to talk to you?'

'You'd like to … I will not be sitting, and you won't be talking. Get up, we're going home.'

'No, Harold, you know how unwell I've been. I can't manage at home.'

Nonsense, such a fuss about nothing. Clara managed perfectly well alone. Your place is with me so gather your things and let's get out before this gets to be fodder for gossip.'

He scooped up the things she'd laid on the dresser and dropped them on the bed.

She ignored him and kept her eyes on the gap in the door, praying that Bella was still listening. 'Harold you must listen to me. I'm not coming back until my baby is born. This is a decent place and you need have no fear that anyone will think poorly of you for providing the nursing I need. You'll be respected for sending me here.'

'For God's sake woman, this is private business between man and wife. What were you thinking coming here to this nest of…?'

His voice was angry, but she realised he was also afraid. Bella was correct, and she should have stood up to him months ago.

'I don't feel safe with you and I'm staying here. If you make a fuss people will think that odd, I suggest you smile and let everyone think this was your idea. When our baby is born, I'll come home.'

'You'll come home now!'

'Shout as loudly as you please, I'm staying here.'

He blustered. 'I won't allow you to shame me, I insist you come home.'

He glanced around the tiny room, 'where's your trunk? We need to get you packed.'

She shook her head. 'Why don't you listen to me for the first time in our marriage?'

His fists clenched. 'Because I'm your husband and you do as I say.'

'You're a bully and a brute, but you won't mistreat me again. I may not be familiar with what occurs between man and wife, but my friends tell me your behaviour is bestial and I'll have no more of it.'

Could that be shame she saw in his eyes? Was she getting through to him?

'Must we discuss this here?'

She was determined to say her piece. 'I'll return when our baby is born, providing I have your word that I'll be treated with respect.'

He rubbed his hands over his face, fingers shaking.

'You'll cause a scandal, this is unnatural behaviour.'

'Even so.'

Reaching out one hand he gripped her upper arm and pulled her close. 'People will talk, you'll be a disgrace.'

'Are you forgetting the thing you've thrown in my face since we married? My low birth, I'm nothing. Who will care what I do?'

'You're mad. You tricked me into marriage and you're trying to trick me now. You've removed my sons from my home without my consent and I'll have the magistrate on you.'

She wiped his spittle from her face with a look of disgust.

The door swung open with a crash and a shadow fell over them both.

'How goes life with you cousin Ellie?' Asked the tall, handsome man who strode in.

The warring husband and wife recognised the visitor at the same time.

'Hugh.' Ellie gasped.

'Mr Daventor.' Harold stammered.

Hugh bent to kiss Ellie and remained with his arm encircling her as he turned to nod politely to Harold.

'Have I interrupted something?' He queried.

'Not at all.'

An inquest was held on Saturday on the body of John Corbett at Clifton upon Teme who, it appeared, had been drinking at the Lion public house in that place a few days since and, having some words on account of gambling with another person there, Robert Wood, the landlord, intervened, put him out of the house and warned him not to enter again.

Corbett, however, insisted on coming back into the house when Wood struck him so violently on the head with a poker as to cause his death a day or so after. Inquest verdict: manslaughter.

CHAPTER TWENTY-SIX

Bella's rich belly laugh echoed round the tiny room. 'Oh, Rube if only you could have seen it. Hugh stood there in his finery tapping the side of his leg with his whip and Ellie sat in the chair and smiled like a lady. Harold goggled like an idiot because he couldn't decide whether to bow or run for his life.'

'But he stayed?'

Bella snorted. 'He wouldn't miss a chance to hob-nob with a Daventor would he? You'd have thought he was talking to the king.'

Ruby poured the tea and nodded happily. 'I knew Hugh would help, but we couldn't see how it could be done. He was all for outright threats and horsewhipping and I'd have gone along with that, but you know Ellie. She'd never have forgiven us. She's hoping once he meets the baby he'll turn decent overnight. Romantic fool.'

'And look where that's got her! But maybe she can hang on to her dream. Hugh looked in control as Harold gabbled on like the half-wit that he is.

'When the fool paused for breath Hugh said, plain as you like, that he knew most of the businessmen for miles around and would be delighted to recommend Harold to his cronies if only he could be certain that cousin Ellie was safe and well.'

Ruby gasped in surprise. 'He was that direct?'

Bella nodded. 'I swear it. Harold's neck swelled up and he turned beet red. He said he wanted no more than Ellie's well-being and he'd make it his life's work to ensure that she flourished.'

It was Ruby's turn to snort. 'He makes my skin crawl, but at least he knows we're on to him and his nasty ways.'

'Oh, he knows. There was no mistaking the message. Ellie's face changed when she realized she had a protector her husband would never dare cross, the frown she's carried for months faded away.

'Hugh kissed her cheek and said he'd walk Harold out to where their horses were stabled. He took his arm and steered him to the door, so I made myself scarce.'

Bella was beaming, a bully had met his match and she'd witnessed it. 'You can stop fretting now, she's safe and has peace of mind. We'll see how she feels after the baby is born and I'll help her do whatever she wants. Now, is there any chance of a bite to eat?'

They went down to Mary, who'd laid out sandwiches and cake for them.

'What news do you have of Richard?' Bella asked, liking her finger to dab up the crumbs.

'He's due to visit today.'

'I'll clear off then.'

'No, stay until he turns up, but don't hold your breath. We haven't seen him for weeks but if he lets us down today I'll have to go and dig him out.

'The twins are taking care of each other in a strange way, but Eliza breaks her heart over him.

'There's not a dive for miles that I don't know about and he won't hide from me for much longer. He can't be allowed to simply forget that he's a father. I'll raise his girls if I must, but they need to know where their Papa is.'

'Hah!' Bella spat, ignoring Mary's scowl. 'He ran for the hills at the first sign of trouble.'

'I'll thank you to remember who you're talking about.'

Bella yawned as though bored. 'I knew you when he was in your belly and I'm not blind to the faults of either of you. You're too full of yourself, and he's spineless. But *we're* here to help you, not get shouted down every time we open our mouths.'

Ruby's eyes darted between the two of them. Bella's jutting chin in direct contrast to Mary's look of shame.

'What do you mean, we? Been talking about me, have you?'

'Well now, as we've been pals since we were little more than children, I'd say yes, we have been talking about. You're in trouble over your head, and we'd like to help. If it suits your ladyship.'

Ruby sat down rubbed her hands over her face, when she looked up her cheeks were burning. 'Sorry, I don't like asking for help, but I may have more on my plate than I bargained for.'

'So, what do you need from us?' Bella asked.

'Knowing you're there helps, but if you can keep an eye on Ellie and Hannah that'd be a load off my mind. Mary's hands are full looking after all of us, although I think I've found the person to help us at home. That'll buy me a bit of time once she's settled. I'll admit, I didn't realise how much hard work three growing girls could be.'

'It's got to be hard for you, not being a natural, motherly type.' Bella said.

'Thanks for that vote of confidence.'

'Well it's true. And don't you be looking down at your shoes Mary, open your mouth and back me up.'

Mary snorted. 'A less maternal woman I've never met, those sad little buggers have her run ragged.'

Bella and Mary roared as Ruby put her hands up in submission. 'It's lucky I've found Juliet then, she's a natural mother hen.'

Mary nodded her agreement as Bella waited for more information.

'The girls adore her already, she's a tiny, pretty little thing, just seventeen and smiling all the time She's the oldest girl at home and has always cared for her younger brothers and sisters.'

'So, she's to be a pal for them?'

Ruby nodded. 'To start with, yes. I want them to know there's someone young on their side. I'm not good at the cuddling thing.'

'I remember the time that fellow tried to…'

'Bella!' Mary hissed.

'Just saying.'

Ruby's lips twitched. 'Nothing can replace what they've lost but she'll help them adjust and, when they're a bit more settled, she'll give them lessons. She can be guided by Ann, but they need someone new and young, just for them.'

Juliet had won her over the moment she'd been introduced to the watchful girls. She'd knelt to enfold Eliza in a hug and smiled at the twins over her head. They'd watched in silence as she loosened one arm and beckoned them in and there they were, all four of them cuddled together.

Juliet spent the day getting to know them and then suggested to Ruby that if she could introduce a fixed daily routine for her to share with them that might help them become friends.

'Things are easing up then?'

Ruby nodded.

The old clock chimed the hour and Bella stood and stretched. 'I'll be on my way, leave the room clear for his highness.'

'And I've work calling me.' Mary said, getting up to leave at the same time.

Ruby kissed them both, one smacker on each cheek.

Ten more days passed before Richard showed himself at Ruby's, by which time she was angry enough to strangle him. It was almost as though he'd waited for the girls to settle down before coming to disrupt them.

During the hour that he spent with them Ruby stomped up and down the hall, determined that he would not leave without explaining himself. She heard him make ready to leave and breezed in and sent the girls out for their walk with Juliet.

She went directly on the attack, raging at him for his neglect of his children, his lack of respect for her and the shameful way he'd deserted Jacob and John at the newspaper.

Her tirade was greeted by silence when she'd expected arguments and excuses.

'Nothing to say, no excuse or apology?' She glared at him, angry enough to shake him.

He was clear eyed and unemotional. 'There's so much I regret, and I wouldn't know where to start putting things right.' He balled his fists until his fingers popped.

'I've been going along with things for years. Running the newspaper, marrying Elizabeth, having the family, building the house. But none of it touched me inside. I've been waiting for something, anything, to matter to me. I'm everything you accuse me of.' He threw his hands up.

'Guilty on all counts and more. I know it, but I don't feel it. I'm empty inside, there's nothing here.' He tapped his chest. 'Nothing.'

His voice was calm, expressionless. The Richard she knew, foolish and slightly lazy, was gone. This stranger left her confused.

'It's my fault Elizabeth and Thomas died. Only that morning I told her I was going to volunteer, this business with France keeps rearing its head and it won't go away. She was shocked and upset and begged me not to go but I knew I had to.'

'You've never expressed any interest in that life!' Ruby snapped. 'You're a newspaper man, a family man, not a soldier. You've been happy in your life, I know you have. This emptiness you talk of, you couldn't have always felt that way.'

'That's almost exactly what she said.' He laughed sadly. 'I am a father, but not a happy one. The girls are very precious, as was Thomas. But that's not enough, I needed to escape. Every day I felt stifled. Can you imagine what that feels like, year after year of feeling nothing but the weight of responsibility and boredom? I was choking on the tedium of it all.'

He shrugged his shoulders in a gesture of defeat and she almost wept. It was the saddest thing she'd ever heard, and to be hearing it from her own son was devastating, but what could she say and how could she make him feel better?

'You felt that way about your family?' She asked.

'I feel that way about my life.'

His pain dispelled her anger. 'The girls will be safe here with me. I'll keep them for you. Go home and take care of your newspaper, forget everything else.'

He shook his head sadly. 'You don't understand, do you? I don't want you to do anything for me!'

She frowned in confusion and he stood up to turn away from her. He moved about the room, picking up a trinket and replacing it, trying to find the words to make her understand.

'Why do you persist in calling me a newspaper man?'

He held his hands up, as though to stop her. 'No, don't answer, let me tell you. I'm a newspaper man because you decided I would be. You bailed out an old friend and earned a slice of his newspaper for your trouble and you decided it would suit me to run it one day when I'd grown up. I don't know what age I was when you made that choice for me, but I was a child, I know that. I was educated and encouraged and told the newspaper would be mine one day, but you never once asked me if that was what I wanted.'

She reached out to put her hand on his shoulder to calm him, but he shook her off, angry now.

'You never ask anyone what they want, you simply roll in and take over. No one has a choice with you.'

He took a deep breath. 'I'm sick of it, I don't want to be your pet newspaper man and I never did. It's your paper, you run it!'

'Business is passed down through families, what a father does, so a son will do. You had no father and Sam had no son, but we were dear friends and he made it his life's work to teach you all he knew, we thought you were happy. Do you have any idea how fortunate you are?'

'Hah, fortune, luck, chance, they don't come into it. We fitted in with your plan. My father was a Daventor, yet canals and gloving play no part in my life because you decided which son got what.'

She clenched her jaw, she despised tears and would not let them fall now. 'That's what families do. I wanted to give you both a future.'

'It wasn't good enough.'

'And so now you'll make your children pay for my sins? You'll turn your back on them and leave them with fearful insecurity. You'll abandon them?'

'You're a fine one to talk of abandonment. Have you forgotten what you did to us all those years ago?'

Guilt churned up inside her, but she tamped it down. 'I've never forgotten my past! You'll never understand why I did the things I did because you don't want to. You've nurtured a feeling of affront that you parade before everyone, using it to justify your own appalling behaviour.

'I explained my reasons to you years ago and there's nothing more I can say. You can keep reminding me for ever, but I did what I thought was right and I will *not* apologise again.'

She cleared her throat. 'You had the best possible chance at life because of the choices I made. If I'd have tried to keep you we'd have starved to death. Ma offered me a fighting chance and I took it, I'm at peace with myself. You come here in your fine clothes and arrogant attitude but with no idea what starvation, or even hunger, feels like because I protected you from it.

'You're not facing what I faced, and I say you cannot desert your children, they need you.'

He reached for the door. 'You did what was best for *you* at the time, now I'm doing the best for *me*. I'm going away, to make something of myself, not something you manipulated others to get for me. I can become someone decent, someone who makes a difference and I intend to.'

'And in the meantime, you're happy for me to bring up your children? Is that the manner of father that you are? I was a terrible mother and yet you'll leave your own flesh and blood with me?'

'They're your flesh and blood too, here's your chance to become a better mother and do for them what you were unable to do for me.'

He laughed bitterly at the look of confusion on her face then he shouted as he left the room. 'Try to love them!'

Her whispered protest went unheard. 'But I *do* love you.'

The Worcester Militia has already turned out a number of fine fellows for the battle-lines overseas and the zeal of volunteering at this moment pervades all classes of this excellent regiment. Viscount Deerhurst, the militia's Lieutenant Colonel (of Croome Court) has, we learn, in the most spirited manner, offered his services to any part of Europe-an example which cannot be too highly rated. It is gratifying to reflect, and must be particularly so to his Lordship's friends, that the comforts and advantages of rank and affluence present no barrier to the fulfilment of that duty which the country requires.
(Copyright and courtesy of the Worcester News)

CHAPTER TWENTY-SEVEN

She sat back, shocked at this worrying development. They'd had countless upsets before, he was as quick to anger as she was, and a heated argument was their usual way of airing differences. This sad and distant stranger was unsettling.

He'd been devastated at the death of his twin and had utterly rejected Ruby, turning to Elizabeth for comfort. It had broken her heart, but she accepted that he was struggling with his emotions.

Since the birth of his children, they'd managed to achieve a reasonably comfortable relationship, they often rowed, but those storms passed, and she'd never doubted that they'd continue in that vein. Now though?

She absently sipped the tea that had been ignored by them both and slammed the cup down with a crack as the cold and slimy brew coated her tongue. She reached instead for the decanter and took such a deep draft of the spirit that her eyes watered.

She had to trust that Richard would come around in time, until then, she must focus on the girls. She sipped the brandy and willed her fighting spirit to raise itself.

There was nothing here she couldn't deal with, she had Juliet and Mary to help in the home and Bella would do all she could. She'd bring up his daughters and she'd educate them and be damned if she didn't provide a future for each of them into the bargain.

If they turned out to be replicas of her, well that would be no more than Richard deserved.

She heard Juliet marshalling them in to lunch and she decided to join them, wanting to be there to support Juliet if they were upset by Richard's. The twins cheerfully told her Papa was going away for a long time on business and that they were to stay here with her and Mary and Juliet.

Ruby nodded. 'I know, that means we'll have to find a room for you to have lessons in.'

They groaned theatrically and even Eliza smiled briefly. She was ghostly pale and sat as close to Juliet as she could, barely uttering a word, but she ate a decent meal and Ruby decided not to interfere.

She watched the twins wolf down their lunch and smiled as Juliet told them to slow down and mind their manners or she wouldn't be taking them out for a walk later. The girl was a treasure and could not be lost.

'I'll be running errands for the rest of the day Juliet, so I'll leave the girls in your capable hands.'

Juliet blushed with pleasure at this sign of trust. 'Of course, Mrs Morgan, don't worry about a thing.'

*The West Worcester Regiment of local militia, having
completed their stated period of training and exercises,
marched hence yesterday. It is but justice to this corps to
say that they have paid every attention to perfecting
themselves in their military discipline and we doubt not
but their exertions will enable them to rank well amongst
the patriotic bands of their countrymen.
(Copyright and courtesy of the Worcester News)*

CHAPTER TWENTY-EIGHT

Ellie held her baby aloft. 'Come and meet your nephew, Aunt Ruby.'

Ruby took the tiny bundle and adjusted the soft blanket to expose more of his face. 'He's lovely, and a hefty weight too. Have you decided on a name for him yet?'

Ellie shrugged. 'Harold wants Percival but I'm not having that. I'll think of something that suits him, but it won't be one Harold chooses.'

'You could do worse than call him Matthew, after our Pa.' She rubbed the downy cheeky and breathed in the smell of him before looking back to her twin. 'You look quite wonderful, so I imagine the pain was all worth it?'

'Pain? Was there pain?' Ellie laughed wearily. Her labour had been long and agonising, both her age and the residual weakness from sickness worked against her.

Lou, fearing for her life, had called on a doctor to help. It took three days to deliver this child and it would be a considerable time before Ellie was fully restored, although her happiness was plain to see.

They admired and petted the baby boy and Ruby watched in fascination as her sister fed him, after which it took only moments for him to settle. He sighed in his sleep and they backed away.

Ruby was direct. 'So, what's next? You know I've got room for you. One or two more will make no difference to us and the boys might be good playmates for my girls.'

Ellie hastily shook her head. 'I've made my bed, as they say. I couldn't leave without the boys, they've already lost their mother. He'd never allow them to stay with me, and he'd take this little one away if he could show I was unfit. That's a battle I can't risk losing.

'He'll behave, he's convinced that with Hugh as a benefactor he'll achieve more success. I don't know all that passed between them, but he refers constantly to *cousin Hugh* and has persuaded himself that he'll soon be elevated to a higher social level. Foolish man!'

Ruby looked down on the sleeping baby then back to her sister. 'And how will it be when he realizes that Hugh has no interest in him whatsoever?' She asked quietly.

'Oh, he knows that now! He's just trying to put a good face on things and if he can make a bit of money into the bargain, so be it. He knows Hugh stepped in to protect me and if he hurts me in any way he'll be destroyed.

'We both know precisely where we stand, and I think it will be the making of us. I'm not afraid of him, Bella convinced me I do hold some power and I need to wield it.'

Ruby's eyes danced with fun. 'That doesn't sound like you, you're usually so mild.'

'Weak, you mean.' Ellie shrugged, seeing the truth in the remark. 'I had several reasons for accepting him. I wanted to be married, I loved his sons and I thought I knew him well enough. I was foolish, why would he select a woman older than himself. He's prosperous and respectable, he could have found a younger, prettier woman!'

She ran her hands over her tired face and glanced ruefully at her reflection before fluffing up her hair and pouting comically. 'I knew it wasn't a love match, but we had our reasons and I imagined we would do well. Most of our reasons are still valid.

'He was savagely angry to discover he wouldn't gain control of Madame Eloise, but that wasn't his only reason for choosing me. He wanted a decent woman to run his home and care for his sons and I'll do that. I've told him I have no intention of sharing his bed again but in all other respects I'll be a good wife and I expect him to be a respectful husband and provider.'

'And if he has other ideas?'

Ellie laughed and put her hands on her hips while trying to scowl aggressively. 'Then I'll kill him in his sleep, with a brick, as Bella first advised.'

They muffled their laughter in a hug.

Ellie pulled away first and wiped her streaming eyes. 'Don't worry about me, I'll be safe and so will my baby.'

Ruby nodded and pecked her sister on the cheek before pulling back.

'Bella was a help to you, was she? I know you two have never seen eye to eye, but I couldn't send Mary, she's too quick to anger, whereas Bella's quick to laugh. I wanted to come myself but with Elizabeth and Thomas...' her voice faltered and here, with her sister, her tears came.

Seeing her new nephew, so soon after losing that dear little boy wrung out her heart. She sobbed once and then the tears began to fall. Ellie leaned against her and rubbed her back as though she were a baby, letting her cry herself out.

The storm was a long time in passing but eventually Ruby lifted her head. 'I'm sorry. I didn't want to bring my grief into this room.'

'Hush. You needed to let it out and if you can't do that with me it's a poor show. Now, there's a basin in the corner, go and splash your face and then we'll take a turn outside with your new nephew. Lou has ordered me to stroll gently, whatever the weather, for fifteen minutes every day and I dare not disobey her. She's small and sweet but she demands obedience. You can meet Harold's boys again for they're out there somewhere.'

They strolled outside and watched a gaggle of children jumping onto frozen puddles in the courtyard. Ellie threaded her arm through Ruby's and looked to the sky, hoping for a little warmth from the sun.

'In answer to your question, Bella was quite wonderful. She's funny and fierce and was quick to give me the benefit of her advice.'

Ruby sniggered and Ellie bit her lip.

'She told me I brought half of my troubles on myself for not putting my foot down. She said he'd have been dead months ago if he'd tried to treat her the way he treated me. I found her bracing.'

Ruby let out a sharp laugh. 'Aye, she's certainly that.'

'She's a good listener, when she stops showing off, and she was strong when I was weak. I owe her a great deal, and I thank you for sending her.'

'I had to do something.'

'What I'm dying to know is how did you get Hugh to step in and help me? I've barely seen him since I left St Johns all those years ago. I was dumbfounded when he turned up to visit me as though we're old friends.'

Ruby thought back to the days when Hugh had been in trouble and turned to her for help, though she'd never breathe a word of that to another soul.

'We've stayed in touch over the years and he calls on me from time to time. I mentioned your situation, trying to clear my own mind really. He said he'd do what he could to help but didn't imagine he'd do as much as he has.'

'Well he's made a world of difference to me.'

Ruby gazed out into the distance. 'I was so afraid for you, you were so clearly sickening but wouldn't say anything so it's good to know you're fighting back.'

Ellie walked over toward a wooden bench and sighed gratefully as she sat down, gesturing Ruby to squeeze in next to her.

'I was ashamed of myself. I was in such a hurry to seize what I thought I wanted that I didn't think it through properly and I landed in a mess. I can't tell you how much I hated myself for being so stupid.'

'It wasn't your fault.' Ruby protested.

'It was my bad judgement, I'm old enough to have known better, and some of it is my own fault. I knew he wouldn't have considered me if he knew about our background. Well, how on earth did I think I could prevent him finding out? I was so desperate to get married that ignored the warning voices in my head.

Then, when it went wrong, I couldn't bear to look at you, to be a disappointment to you.'

'I came to you once before and you helped me rebuild my life, I couldn't burden you with something I brought on myself.'

Ruby put her arms gently around her sister. 'There was no need for shame, not on your part. I'll be there for you if ever you need me, and I know you'd do the same for me. Sisters can't ever be burdens. '

'Well anyway, I have my beautiful son, so I can't completely regret marrying him, and I do believe we can carry on together. We'll simply write our own rules for our marriage. All I require from him now is a little distance.'

Ruby smiled grimly. 'We'll be watching him though, you can be sure of that.'

'That makes me feel even more secure. Now then, we've talked more than enough about me. Tell me your news, I want to hear about Richard and his girls. Tell me all.'

'Richard has stopped drinking thankfully. I was terrified that habit might stick with him. But I do have a tale to tell.' She brought Ellie up to date.

'He's already gone?' Ellie gasped.

Ruby nodded. 'He's over in Witley where there's some secret experiment going on. He's bought himself a commission and will be trained to use a rifle. They're taking anyone who can pay their own way. He's promised to keep in touch, but I set no store by that. He's going off to be a hero, which is something he's showed no desire for in the past.'

'War, for men it's always war!'

Ruby admitted that little else was being talked of, written about in the London papers. The expected invasion of Napoleon and his men had everyone afraid to one degree or another.

'George Coventry's got over seven hundred volunteers signed up and they'll be marching off to Gosport as soon as he's got them knocked into shape. They've stopped all grazing on Pitchcroft and he's got the run of the place to train his men.

'But there's not a word being said about Witley so I don't know what to think about that.'

'Is an invasion really likely?'

'Well, nobody knows for sure, but we'll be ready if the worst comes to the worst. Men the length of the country are training, and their women are turning out rag-tag uniforms. It feels serious to me.'

'Why can we never learn?'

'God help the French if they do set foot in England, you never saw such a rough looking bunch of no-goods as are strutting about like they're already bloody heroes. They're running amok, no half decent inn will let them through their door, every night there's a fight somewhere.

'George Coventry reckons he's almost got them ready for battle, but the way they're carrying on they'll kill each other before the French attack. Bloody rabble! And Richard's one of them.'

'He'll be home when he's ready Ruby, you know he's always been... '

'I know what he's always been, and I'm not going to worry about him anymore. I have his children to think of. He can take care of himself.'

'And how are you liking it, living with them?' Ellie couldn't really picture her sister as a doting mother to a brood of girls.

'Well, the noise and the mess are beyond my understanding. Since Juliet came to us, they squeal and fight, they can't walk but must run. I'm pleased really, because when they first came they didn't make a sound and I was worried sick. They're almost back to normal and they're wearing me out.'

She looked at Ellie, her eyes sad. 'It's all so different to when I had my babies. I could weep for the child I was, and the choices I had to make.'

She gazed off, re-living the day Ma told her she must give up her boys if she wanted to stay with her. She was ashamed of the relief she remembers feeling then.

'You did what you had to do Ruby. No-one thinks the worse of you.'

'Oh no, I had no choice, but I do think a more natural woman might have suffered more than I did at giving them up. I was glad to be free of them, and I'd be a liar to deny it. I'll do a better job this time or die trying.'

Ellie hoped the girls would be able to heal her damaged sister. 'No-one's judging you, Ruby.'

'Richard is, but I understand that. He can't imagine what it was like for me back then, there's no reason he should. The girls are a fresh start for me, I love them dearly and I'm scared to death I'll get it wrong. I swear I'd kill anyone who threatened them, I really would. God knows, they've disrupted my life beyond belief, but I'm ready for more.'

'So, here we are, at an age when we should be grandmothers, embarking on motherhood.' Ellie spoke with wonder in her voice.

'We are that. Now then, call over the boys so I can meet them, and I'll leave you to rest. Send me a message before you return home though, I want to come with you.'

'Ruby, there's no need.'

'But I'll come anyway. Promise me?'

Ellie nodded and beckoned the two small boys who were watching them. Samuel and Simon Pargeter were sturdy boys with ruddy complexions and dark watchful eyes that were quick to smile. They answered shyly when Ruby asked them their names, but it was clear that though they might be timid with strangers they had no qualms at all when dealing with Ellie. They romped and teased with her and she was clearly in her element.

Ruby left them playing together happily.

On Sunday last James Hutchins, a private in the Worcester Local Militia, was apprehended as a deserter for not having joined the regiment on its first assembling. He was on Monday sentenced to hard labour in our House of Correction for six months. We trust this will operate as a warning to local militiamen not joining their regiments.
(Copyright and courtesy of the Worcester News)

CHAPTER TWENTY-NINE

Seeing her proudly confident sister and healthy new nephew put Ruby in a calmer, more positive mood. Having talked out her worries and cried like a fool had cleared a lot of rubbish from her head.

She made an unscheduled stop at Sansome Springs, startling Barnabus who abandoned his accounts ledger as soon as he saw her. They chatted as they ambled through the gardens. She listened to his every word though her eyes were never still, darting from side to side and missing nothing. Everywhere was as neat and tidy as it had ever been and by the time they reached the spring, she was satisfied he had things under control.

'Show me what you envisage here.' She gestured to the spring. 'I want you describe what I could see if your plans were put in place.'

He strode enthusiastically back and forth, pointing here there and everywhere as he relayed the details. He'd thought of everything she had and more, he had ready answers to all her questions, though he had to think about the final one.

'Tell me this, *if* I agreed with your plan and put you in charge of the project, when do you think the work should begin?'

His eyes widened but he gained control of himself very quickly. She watched his lips move as he considered his response.

'We should begin right away. There are few visitors now and that gives us the opportunity to get a considerable amount done with minimal disruption.'

He walked up and down again, running things through his mind. 'I'll need screens to hide the work, and I'd want them to illustrate what we're building. It will whet their appetites and guarantee us a good show when we open.'

She nodded thoughtfully, he'd considered the opening already, a good sign. 'Have you ordered the screens?'

'Not without your blessing.'

'Then I suggest you send word to Dennis without delay, though I suspect he'll be one step ahead of you. He'll have drawings and ideas ready for you to see. Decide what you want, then go ahead.'

He looked at her uncertainly and she stepped forward to touch his elbow. 'I'm eager to see what you can do here so, get things moving as quickly as you can. Keep this in mind, I have every confidence in you, but if you need advice, or a second opinion and don't want to approach me, Ben, Francis and Dennis can be relied on. I don't want you to feel overwhelmed.'

'I'm honoured that you've listened to my ideas and have agreed to have this… glasshouse, built. I won't disappoint you. I'm so...' his words tumbled out in a torrent.

'Enough.' She put her hands up in a gesture of submission and laughed. 'You'll be working harder than ever before, so no more thanks. You have a great deal of thinking to do.'

'Yes, of course.'

'I'll expect you to continue to visit me each week to keep me in the picture. I don't want to hear anything from the gossips until I've heard it from you. Clear?'

He nodded.

'And by the way, I hate the word glasshouse. Let's find a better name before it sticks.'

'I agree. I've something in mind, but I'd like to check a few more details before we adopt a title, if you can bear with me.'

'I've got my hands full to overflowing so you take your time. We need to get it right, that's the key.'

They shook hands and she left without a backward glance. He had facts and figures at his fingertips and his nerves were no longer getting the better of him. He'd grown well into his new position and she could leave him to flourish.

He watched her go, his heart pounding. As soon as she was out of sight he dropped to his haunches sucked in his breath. She'd shocked him this time.

He flopped back on the grass and let out a shout of laughter. It took him a good half hour to get his head straight. This was his chance to really impress her and he wouldn't fail.

At least the workers here would be on his side, he'd had to win them over when Ruby had handed management over to him. A few worked from years back were awkward and he'd feared a mutiny, at the last minute someone saw sense and spoke up for him.

'Give the lad a chance, he works as hard as any of us and he's a bloody sight easier to please than she is at times.'

There were a few grumbles before a woman's voice piped up. 'Aye, and he don't have her wicked temper, that's for sure.'

That started a gradual shift in attitude and now he was almost as confident in his management as Ruby was. But this was huge. How could he manage such a vast project alone, and what would happen if he spoiled her gardens?

Well, he knew. She'd kill him.

The village of Great Malvern has proved more attractive than usual this season, Among recent arrivals are Lord and Lady Calthorp, Lady Headely, Sir James and Lady Graham, Lady Cranley and General Lefevre.
(Copyright and courtesy of the Worcester News)

CHAPTER THIRTY

Having two successful visits under her belt had given Ruby a lift and she decided to check up on Harold before her last visit of the day.

The approach was freshly swept, and the windows sparkled in the watery sun. A bell tinkled prettily as she opened the door of the shop that bore the sign *Pargeter and Sons, Apothecary and Perfumier.* There being no sign of Harold, she withdrew, slightly deflated. She tried to set eyes on him at least once a day, in part to remind him she was watching, and partly for the pleasure of seeing his impotent hatred.

She rang the bell of Madame Eloise, this was the venture that could present problems she couldn't resolve. She knew nothing of the world of beauty and cared less but was determined Ellie's husband never got his hands on it. She'd raze it to the ground first.

She saw only two options, if Hannah could continue without Ellie, well and good, if not, the business would close.

A maid ushered Ruby into the comfortable waiting room and invited her to have a seat as she went to see if Hannah was available. Ruby smiled at her efforts, she knew Hannah expected her visit and would be free, but she admired the exclusive gloss this little concern had coated itself with.

The waiting room was small, with a large window letting in plenty of light. The pictures on the walls depicted women through the ages at their toilette. A pretty, round, wooden table was buffed to a high shine and it held two of the London periodicals devoted to fashion. There was a tiled fireplace with a cheerful fire that warmed the room and released the perfume from the basket of lavender and rosemary placed nearby. The drapery and rugs were of muted colours and the mood was calm and comforting.

When she'd taken over the building the ground floor had been one large room that Ellie wanted divided into two smaller rooms. This was one half, the other half faced the rear and was were where Ellie and Hannah perfected the lotions, potions and pomades that had made their name.

Everything they used was prepared by them, from minute patches of mouse fur to add fullness to thin eyebrows, beet juice for blushing up pale cheeks and burnt candle-wick to darken fair lashes. They had lengths of horsehair that could be inserted into intricate hairstyles to give the illusion of a greater crowning glory whilst chicken skin gloves soaked in lemon could help whiten the hands.

Ellie and Hannah liked nothing more than concocting lotions and waters and testing them on friends and family until they had an answer to almost every female need. They'd built up a list of ladies who placed regular orders for the products that were tailor-made for them and a young boy was employed to deliver these orders.

The maid returned and guided Ruby up the stairs and into one of the private salons on the middle floor, as her door closed she heard a woman exiting another of these sanctums and go softly down the stairs.

This system ensured privacy for clients and had proved golden for Madame Eloise whose patrons came from the peak of Worcester society. No word had ever escaped that would cause any society dame to blush.

King George had decried such practices as witchcraft and trickery, but everyone knew he was a bloody madman and there were precious few women about who did not employ some method or another to improve her looks, whether anyone knew and approved, or not.

Hannah bustled in, straightening her apron. She was thinner than Ruby remembered and there was an air of distraction about her.

'Sorry I kept you waiting, my customer needed a few extra moments to talk about her daughter.'

Ruby waved away her apology. 'It's me that should be apologising leaving you here to carry on alone. If you need to attend to someone else, do. No need to stand on ceremony with me.'

Hannah lowered herself into a seat and sighed with pleasure. 'No-one's expected for the rest of the day, it generally starts off brisk in the mornings but falls off through the afternoon in the cold weather. I usually stop for tea about this time and then I'll spend an hour or so preparing for tomorrow after I make up the orders that are due to be delivered.'

She followed Hannah up a shorter set of stairs into the attic room she'd shared with Ellie for years and saw at once that these rooms were not nearly as comfortable as the waiting room.

The best of everything had been provided for the customers and Hannah was making do with inferior furniture and no decorations or softness of any description. Her room was depressing and shabby, and very cold.

There were two curtained off alcoves at the far side which had served as bedrooms for Hannah and Ellie, who'd lived here from the beginning, until Ruby had asked them to move into the house she'd bought in Foregate.

They'd done as she'd asked and moved in to the house she was using to train girls for domestic service. She'd hope their core of satisfied customers would help spread the word for her.

Richard's words echoed in her head. *You never ask anyone what they want, you just roll in and take over their lives.* She had an uncomfortable realisation that he'd been correct in his accusations. It wouldn't hurt to consider those around her now and again.

When Ellie had decided to wed she'd moved out of the training house into her new husband's home and Hannah had quietly come back here to these depressing rooms and Ruby had not spared her a moment of thought.

After laying out the simple tea, the maid left quietly, and Ruby had a memory of herself doing the same thing for Ma. She remembered scuttling about, in fear of her future. Nowadays she had people to lay her own tea out and thought nothing of it. She decided to seek her out when her business was finished and thank her.

Hannah spoke the instant the maid closed the door, asking anxiously after her friend. 'Have you seen Ellie and the baby?'

'I was with them first thing and they're both well. She's tired but the baby is a chubby little fellow who has already got her enchanted. She wanted me to thank you for all you've done. She's itching to see you and introduce her baby.'

'Oh, I'm that pleased, it's been such a worrying time. I've been beside myself fretting about her and what I should do for the best. What will she do now though, has she said? If you don't mind me asking.'

'Ellie has no secrets from you and I know how concerned you've been about her. Her plans are to come back home, she feels able to cope better now but I'll let her tell you more when you see her.'

Hannah nodded her head in satisfaction. 'Those boys don't need to lose another mother. A secure home is everything.'

Ruby moved on to business. 'You've been sadly neglected here and for that I owe you an apology. Things have been difficult for my family for some quite time, but that's no excuse for deserting you.'

Hannah's hand covered her mouth. 'I'm awful sorry about Elizabeth and the baby, my mind has been on Ellie, but you've had terribly things to deal with. I don't know how you've coped. I'm so thoughtless.'

Ruby smiled at her kindness. 'Truly Hannah, I could give you lessons in thoughtlessness, but let's hope I can make amends. I want you to tell me how I can best help.'

As Hannah picked at a sandwich Ruby was considering her own neglect of this business. 'Hannah, do you realise we opened Madame Eloise twenty years ago?'

'As much as that, twenty years. Well.' Hannah quickly swallowed her sandwich.

'Yet in all that time you've never asked for anything, more money, better living conditions, or more help. Why is that?'

Hannah picked up a tiny cake and looked at it closely before replacing it. 'When I found out I was having a baby, my mother told me I'd ruined my life and should expect nothing good to ever happen to me again.'

Ruby knew what that felt like.

'I came to you in desperation and you took me in and kept safe, after the baby you found me decent work. You said. *I can see you're made for something different.* You never complained or reminded me what I owed you, you offered me the chance to come here and learn from your sister.

'You're the miracle that saved my life, how could I *ever* ask you for more?' Hannah was flushed and her hand trembled as she wiped away a tear.

Ruby swallowed hard and blinked her own smarting eyes. She took a sip of her tea, craving a shot of something to liven it up. Then she laughed. 'I've been called many things, but that's first time I've been called a miracle.'

Hannah simply shrugged. 'You're a miracle to me.'

'I was in the same position when Ma saved me, and she still has the blackest name in town though she's been dead for years. I always saw her as my guardian angel and wouldn't hear a bad word about her. After she got sick I was able to re-pay her in hard work and care, and you've paid me back in the same coin. But at the same time, I had a great inheritance from Ma at the end. It's only right that I do something better for you. Twenty years of hard work deserves a reward.'

'I don't need more Ruby, I do good work and I'm paid fairly. I can hold my head up, that's worth more than anything.'

'You deserve better living accommodations for a start. I'm appalled at the state of these rooms. The two lower floors are perfect, but this should be as good, if not better for you. I don't want you to be here alone at night, I should be whipped for allowing that to go on. Not to mention the extra work that you're doing. How long will putting up the orders for delivery take?'

'A couple of hours, Jessie's good, she's young, but she's quick, and is a great help to me. And I haven't been alone, Ellie and I worked together every day until she got sick. You have enough to think about, don't you worry about me.' Hannah said anxiously.

'Ellie won't be coming back to work for a long time though, if at all. She's not strong, and she has a family that will take most of her time. Madame Eloise has to change.'

Hannah cried out in distress. 'I can keep it all going Ruby, don't close us down, it's my life.'

'Madame Eloise will be yours for as long as you want it. I simply want to give you some help. I think two young girls, lively and bright that you can train up, slowly. Nice girls that you'll be happy living with, perhaps they can share what used to be Ellie's room.

'You'll have company then, day and night, and gradually you'll be able to have a bit of a rest. If I were you I'd keep working with Jessie as well, if you like her then in a few years she might be able to do more.'

Hannah didn't speak but the look of gratitude on her face was answer enough.

'I'm going to start looking for those girls straight away, I've got a couple in my mind that are back at my house in training. You'll need to meet them. *You* must select your helpers, not me.'

Hannah nodded, her head was whirling, she'd feared her work was to be taken away from her and now it seemed it was all getting better.

'I'm going to arrange for Mr Williams to tell us what can be done to improve up here for you.'

'It would be wonderful.' Hannah chirped up at last. 'I'd love to have someone else living here and younger girls would cheer me up. I feel as though I haven't laughed for a very long time.' She sat up straighter and her eyes sparkled with excitement now she trusted her work would continue and she'd have some company at nights.

'I suggest you gather your things together and come back to stay in my house for the time being. That will leave these rooms empty for Mr Williams to get started as quickly as he can. I really don't want you to spend another night alone here.'

Hannah protested. 'I'm not always alone, Jessie stays when she can, but she has to do a lot to help her mother.'

'Then Jessie can go home to her mother, I want you to have other people around you until we have nicer apartments here for you and your new assistants.'

Hannah nodded her head as she dashed tears from her eyes. 'I'll make up the orders and come along later if that's what you want.'

Ruby wrapped her arms around her in a moment of intimacy that took them both by surprise.

Ruby was not used to showing affection but the events of the last few months had taught her that there were things about herself she'd do well to change.

If Hannah was the first to feel the benefit, she wouldn't be the last.

Number 57 High Street Worcester. R Lewis, linen draper, haberdasher and hosier begs leave to inform the ladies of Worcester and its vicinity that he has selected from the first markets, a large and extensive assortment of the goods in which he trades, well adapted for the present season.

He is determined to sell some of the greatest bargains ever offered to the public, including prints and ginghams from 6d a yard, white calico from 4d a yard, pocket handkerchiefs and black stockings from 12d a pair.

(Copyright and courtesy of the Worcester News)

CHAPTER THIRTY-ONE

Despite the biting cold, The Foregate was teeming with life by the time Ruby headed home. She smiled at mothers who screeched at scruffy children too busy scuffling and fighting to hear. Chickens and dogs tormented each other between the legs of plodding horses, tired at the end of a day's work. A group of old men sat on a crumbling stone wall and watched it all pass by.

Two lads exchanged cross words but neither had the stomach to exchange blows. A wiry delivery boy grinned as he picked his way around them, anxious to deliver his last package of the day, meanwhile the cook shops threw open their doors and the air was filled with the smells of the food that had been cooking for hours.

This was what Ruby thrived on, the hustle and bustle of humanity rubbing along together as the smells and sounds of life, with all its possibilities, enveloped all. The atmosphere woke her up and put a spring in her step and on days like these she felt equal to anything and everything. She took one last glance around the lively outdoor scene and approached her front door, anticipating a quiet evening with Mary re-capping the events of her hectic day.

As the door opened she was hit by a blast of squealing and the thunder of thudding footsteps. Mary poked her head around the kitchen door, eyes rolling and looking distinctly unimpressed.

'Is Juliet unwell?'

'Probably, the bloody noise is making me sick.' Mary smirked and closed the door.

Ruby climbed the stairs, fearing she was about to find a revolution taking place. Juliet was a stickler for an hour of peace and quiet before bed and this noise would not be to her liking.

Opening the door of the playroom she saw a crowd of children piled into a heap on the floor. Juliet stood to one side, hopelessly outnumbered and looking a little tearful. She flushed to crimson red when Ruby entered the room.

The melee slowly shifted and then separated into individual children, all of whom had been clambering on the man who lay on his back at the heart of the scene. He pulled himself up to his full height and grinned.

'Ah Ruby, I apologise. Your wonderful Juliet tried to keep us calm but I'm afraid we were having too much fun.'

Ruby shook her head in mock exasperation. 'Hugh, I didn't expect you. Did I?'

'No, no.' He put his hands up in a gesture of apology. 'I called in on a whim, bad manners I know but I felt it was beyond time my brood got to know yours. And we are family, are we not?'

Ruby walked over to Juliet and squeezed her arm reassuringly. 'Don't worry, this will not become a habit.'

Her gaze swept over the giggling romp of children. Boys were racing the length of the room as the girls squealed encouragement, it was pure chaos and the noise was beyond enduring, but her three girls were laughing and racing about like normal children and she felt her heart melt.

'Just tonight.' She said to Juliet, who was looking happier now she saw that Ruby didn't hold her responsible.

She enjoyed watching the fun for another half an hour before calling a halt. 'Hugh, it's getting late, they'll never sleep.'

He stood at once and clapped his hands. 'Enough now! Help tidy this room up and I don't want to hear a sound from any of you. Juliet will be here to watch you while I step outside for a moment.' He looked at each child individually, nodded his head once and left the room.

Ruby followed him, amazed that he got the obedience he clearly expected from her girls in addition to his children.

She breathed a sigh of relief. 'I'm happy to see you, truly, but today has been long and I'm very tired.'

'It was selfish of me to call so late. But I've hardly seen you, you've so much deal with, and I thought strength in numbers.' He looked contrite, so much like her playmate of old that she laughed.

'You *are* family, and the girls need to know children their own age, and to see them laughing and rolling about was wonderful. It reassures me that they'll be alright.'

'Oh, they will. Believe me, children are tough little brutes. Tell me about your day?'

'I've seen Ellie, Barnabus and Hannah, in that order, and I have a lot to think about.'

'Aha, so you've met your new nephew?'

She smiled. 'He's bonny, and she's smitten. Thank you for helping her.' She gestured to a chair and he made himself comfortable.

'I'm happy to have been able too, but really, what was she thinking, marrying a toad like him? He's a chancer with a very thin veneer of decency.' He smiled as he took the drink she handed him and watched as she pondered her answer.

'She wanted to be married and have her own family so badly, and then, when she thought it was too late, he proposed. She didn't think it through properly.'

'Well, I'll keep an eye on him. I'll never forget what I owe you and I'm happy to do this for you.'

'All debts are paid Hugh. Can we simply go on as friends?'

He nodded, and she smiled.

'Good. Let's have another drink and you can tell me your news, though I can't promise not to fall asleep on you.'

He laughed. 'Next time I call I'll make it earlier in the day and bring fewer children with me.'

'Bring who you like. It's not your fault that I've been so tied up today.'

'We're on our way home and I called in on impulse. I'm trying to keep the children out in the late afternoons to allow Gweneth some quiet time. She'd prefer them to have a governess and be in a classroom, but I think fresh air and seeing a bit of the world is better for them. I had business in town and I thought it would be an adventure to bring them over the river with me. It was always such a thrill for us, do you remember?'

Ruby laughed. 'I recall looking at Worcester from St Johns and longing to be able to cross over and explore. It was always a place of enchantment for me.'

He nodded his understanding. Ruby had been the instigator of adventure and trouble for them all as children. She'd been fearless, and he'd learned a lot from watching her. He regretted the years of their estrangement and was determined not to lose her again.

She felt his eyes on her and asked pointedly, 'how is Gweneth?'

The two women were never to be more than passing acquaintances, both disapproving of the other, but remaining cordial for Hugh's sake.

Gweneth came from a well set up family and took pride in her marriage to the son of a noted family. She strived daily to drive their position in society upwards and for a time, he'd gone along with her, wanting her to be happy. The death of Tom changed the way he viewed everything, and he was motivated to rekindle his childhood friendship with Ruby, against his wife's wishes.

Hugh nodded amiably. 'She's well, but she needs her rest.'

Ruby raised her eyebrows in question and he nodded a little ruefully.

'We'll have another child shortly.'

'The poor woman.' Ruby said with feeling.

Hugh looked shocked for a moment and then bellowed out a laugh. 'No-one but you would be so blunt. I'll admit, I'm a bit daunted by the thought of having our sixth child.'

'Well, it's not something she did on her own, thank goodness she's a born mother, she'll cope.'

'Yes indeed.' He agreed briskly. 'We're making changes though. I'm having a larger house built out at Bransford. We're cramped already at home and it's something we've talked of for a long time. She'd like to be further away from the works and to have space to keep a few horses for the children.'

Ruby looked at her friend, the boy she had loved so much as a girl. 'Earlier today Ellie remarked on us both embarking on motherhood at a late age and here you are, keeping step. Have we become old Hugh?'

'Older maybe, never old Ruby, not us!'

In due course Hugh marshalled his children out into the dark night after promising the young cousins could get together once a week.

Juliet smiled weakly at this news, but Ruby assured her that gaining a handful of cousins was a great thing and must be encouraged. The girl went gratefully to bed, preferring solitude over supper.

As silence fell over the house Ruby and Mary pulled their chairs closer to the fire and settled down to mull over the day.

Mary kept herself behind the scenes when company was around, more comfortable in the kitchen than the parlour. Ruby found it easy to move between high and low society, Mary, like Ma, was determined to stay where she felt safest.

But these two women were most things to each other, advisers, comforters, friends and so much more. Neither Ellie nor Bella could divide them.

Together they were peaceful and content, when Bella joined them she brought the spark that turned them raucous, made them laugh and encouraged them to keep sampling the delights that pleased them most.

As Ruby held onto Mary's work roughened hand she reflected that all the Ellies' and Gweneths' and Elizabeths' in the world would never make her regret meeting and loving Mary, and dearest Bella.

How she was going to balance that messy life and those loves, with the bringing up of three small girls she had no idea, but she didn't doubt she'd manage it.

She smiled wickedly to think of the grand Elizabeth spinning in her grave at the very thought.

Great preparations are in the making for the celebration of our Musical Festival at Worcester on the 27th, 28th and 29th. The scheme of the different performances presents a selection, fully calculated to display to the utmost extent the vocal harmony of the soloists and chorus.

The major works in the programme include Handels's sacred oratorio The Messiah.
(Copyright and courtesy of the Worcester News)

CHAPTER THIRTY-TWO

Jacob and John kept their eyes down and their mouths shut as Ruby tutted and sighed and tore out her hair at the confusion that consumed the newspaper office. They were continuing to produce the newspaper, but the records were not being accurately kept and the accounts were a mess. She was seriously considering closing the thing down.

Ann was in a fighting mood which made the atmosphere even more fraught. 'This newspaper has been established for 150 years and we have a duty to continue. We're highly valued and are not running at a loss. I don't know what your problem is, but I wish you would stop looking for trouble.'

Ruby pushed her hair back from her face and sighed deeply. 'I'm not looking for trouble, but I can't be here every day. I hardly spend any time at all with the girls and that's something I vowed I would do. I'm being torn into too many pieces.'

The strain she felt was real. She was deathly pale except for the black shadows beneath her eyes and, although she'd never carried excess weight, she was now skeletal.

Ann braced herself to hand out some home truths. 'The newspaper does need help, I'll agree with that but what it does *not* need is you interfering.'

Ruby was caught off guard. 'Well perhaps you would be good enough to tell me what you do need then.' She tossed the sheaf of papers in her hand on to the heaped desk. 'You're in a mess here and I won't allow that to continue. Frankly I think you're beyond saving.'

'I haven't spanked you since you were six years old Ruby Morgan, but I swear I'm as close as I've ever been to giving you a lathering. You've offended me, and insulted the boys, which is unforgivable. They have so much respect for you and are working incredibly hard to fill the gap that Richard left behind. You accused him of being lazy and careless, but he's left a void here and you're not helping. Day after day you pick holes in our work, destroying their confidence and driving me to distraction. I'm sick of hearing you tell me how much better we should be doing the things that we've been doing well enough for years.'

She inhaled deeply and rushed on. 'None of us are clerks or managers. You least of all. Heaven knows I've heard you claim often enough that you can tell at a glance if a business is profitable, but you don't understand our system, you don't know how newspapers work and you're getting in our way.'

Ruby's face was thunderous, but Ann hadn't finished. 'What we need is a clerk, a quiet, efficient man who will restore the system we originally had. It worked well until you came along and made your improvements.'

'Are you asking me to believe that *Richard* was your clerk?' Ruby asked in disbelief.

Ann shook her head in denial. 'No, I was the clerk. But nowadays I'm trying to guide Jacob as he attempts to fill Richard's shoes out in the real world, and that takes time.

'He's a young man, struggling to take on what Richard grew up doing, and he's doing it very well. Or he was until he was forced to listen to you, day after day, talking about how badly we're doing.'

Ruby was crushed, she'd been desperately trying to think of what to do for the best and it hadn't occurred to her that she was part of the problem. She was learning some hard life lessons. 'I've made things worse, have I?' She asked quietly.

Ann wasn't ready to let her off the hook just yet. 'Yes, you have.'

Ruby was always so certain that she knew best and the less she knew the more stubborn she became. Ann had to stop her before the damage was irreparable.

'I try to get in here at night, once I know Jacob is set up. But each day I find you've moved something or sent a letter out to an advertiser and caused offence, and I can't keep up with it. What I really need is for you to stop helping.'

'I didn't know.' Ruby protested.

'You didn't ask!'

'I'm sorry.'

'Yes. Well, now you know.'

Ann planted her hands on her hips and Ruby decided to back off. 'I'll go and make some tea and then I'll leave you to it.'

It was a good hour later that Ruby banged the little gong that announced that tea was made. They gathered together around the massive old table and when they all had a drink she told them she'd be leaving the management of the newspaper in Ann's capable hands.

Ann nodded approval, and Jacob and John held their breath. Ruby had given them a home and work and they loved her for it, but she was nightmare to work with and the sooner she buggered off, the happier they'd be.

Ann escorted Ruby to the door, determined to get rid of her.

'I don't remember you ever spanking me Ann.' Ruby remarked with a smile.

'Well, there's my mistake! Now go. I'll send a message if we need help. Otherwise Jacob will be along to present the report in a few weeks. And just remember, he's filling shoes he never expected to fill so give the lad a chance. You won't find a better, or more loyal worker than him but he needs to know you appreciate him.'

'Bless you Ann.'

Ruby trudged up the hill toward the cathedral in a reflective mood. She had genuinely thought she was helping and had been dreading closing the newspaper down. That she was causing damage was Richard's criticism come to life. How she wished she'd taken the time to tell him that she was proud of him instead of constantly criticising his efforts.

The sun shone and, thinking the air would do her good, she took a detour through the cathedral grounds and thought of her mentor, Sam Thatcher. He'd walk from the offices up here whenever he needed space to think, he always said thinking was as important as doing, and so often he'd urged her not to rush headlong into things.

She winced at how heavy handed she'd been. It had been quite a leveller to realise that she was not held in the esteem that she'd imagined she was. Ann had put her firmly in her place. She was fortunate to be surrounded by strong people.

She was diverted by the sound of a band striking up as she crossed the green to come alongside the Guild Hall, the new market hall was being formally opened that day.

For as long as she could remember, traders had set their stalls out on the tracks and alleyways of Worcester in the spot that their fathers and grandfathers before them had set up shop. Everyone knew who was where, what they sold and when they would be back.

She'd grown used to seeing them and enjoyed their convenience, but they'd been falling out of favour for a long time. There was no control on what they sold or on the mess they left behind when their work was done.

Certainly, she avoided The Cross when she could, choosing to take a longer route rather than risk her life walking where wagons and stalls choked the tracks.

Livestock frequently broke free from their makeshift pens, and though chasing them was great fun for children, housekeepers were up in arms as clean laundry was often ripped off the bushes it had been spread across to dry. The devastation that a trapped animal could do to a kitchen garden was staggering.

The locals had protested for long enough and this new market hall was the solution.

She decided to see what it had to offer while it was still shiny and new. At the front were rows of fruit and vegetable stalls, their owners standing beside them, looking self-conscious and out-of-place but proud at the same time.

In the row behind them were bakers and pastry cooks. Ruby inhaled deeply as she passed by. Surely nothing smelled sweeter than freshly baked bread.

At the very back of the market hall were the butchers whose stalls backed onto the Shambles, the depository for blood and offal. Here the air was thick with the steam of hot blood and animal waste and she quickly wrapped her shawl around her nose and mouth, thankful that Mary did their shopping and cooking.

She hastened away and paused near the men selling fabrics, ribbons and lace work, and fancy goods, as the marching band entered the space.

Music echoed around the vaulted ceiling, ending all conversation. Small boys followed the band around the hall and Ruby stayed to enjoy the opening ceremony, feeling proud of her enlightened city.

Notice is hereby given that for the protection of all persons attending Worcester market with provisions of every description, the major and justices of the City have sworn in an extra number of constables who, if occasion should require, will give their assistance to prevent the interruption of the sale thereof by any evil-disposed person or persons.

(Copyright and courtesy of the Worcester News)

CHAPTER THIRTY-THREE

The cries of a new-born baby broke the tension that had hung over the house in St Johns for days. Hugh jumped to his feet but remained where he was, he'd be no use up there and he needed to talk to the doctor.

Hearing the heavy footsteps on the stairs he poured a couple of drinks and handed one to the medical man as he walked in. The doctor sighed his appreciation and swirled the biting spirit around his mouth before swallowing.

'Your son is small but may rally. Sadly, the same cannot be said for Mrs Daventor… she's suffered greatly and I'm afraid…' He shook his head and gazed into his empty glass.

Hugh coughed and gulped down the spirit, trying to make sense of what he'd just heard. 'She's had a difficult time of it, I know, but surely she simply needs to rest?' He managed.

The doctor shook his head. 'I'm sorry Hugh, it's unlikely. It was too much for a woman of her age and sensibilities, there's nothing to be done for her apart from prayer I'm afraid.'

'My son?'

The doctor continued to shake his head pessimistically and it took all Hugh's strength to not thump the fool. 'He's small and weak you see. And without his mother… I'm sorry.'

'I'll be back tomorrow to see how they do, but I'm not optimistic. You'll need a nurse to stay, I know of a good woman if you'd like my advice?'

Hugh nodded absently. 'Of course, whatever you say. If you'll be so good as to arrange it.'

'I'll send her along to you tomorrow. For tonight have a maid stay in the room with her, she shouldn't be left alone.'

He glanced to the window in irritation at the sound of the children playing outside. 'And do try to keep them quiet, she needs peace.'

Pompous idiot, children had to run and play, surely the man understood that. Hugh allowed the manners that had been instilled in him to take over and he nodded politely and shook the man's hand before closing the door on him. What was the point of paying for a doctor? They had little idea what they were doing and were useless when something went wrong.

He called out to the children to play quietly, then he walked up the stairs. He had a new son to meet, a sick wife to nurse and five demanding children to care for. He stepped into his wife's room, unable to hide his distaste at the heat and sour smell.

Gweneth lay pale and insubstantial and he felt a shudder of fear pass through him, she was barely recognisable. The maid attempted to wipe her face with a cool cloth, but she tossed and turned dreadfully. At least the woman seemed gentle and she spoke softly.

The baby lay quietly in a cot beside the bed and Hugh picked him up and cradled him gently, bending over so the boy and his Mama were almost face to face, but this unsettled Gweneth who moaned and tried and turn away. He lay the baby back in his bed and held a whispered conversation with the maid who assured him she could manage both mother and baby for one night.

Even as he nodded his appreciation, he could hear the shouts and screams of his children outside.

He'd have to find someone to help with the children and they were an unruly bunch. Both he and their mother doted on them and had spoiled them, and although *he* could manage them, he knew of no-one else who could.

He had a reliable household staff but not one of them had ever got the better of his children, they were wild and had always depended on Mama for forgiveness for all their tricks and pranks.

His own childhood had been spent under the care of his uncle, and he'd lived in fear of offending him and being sent away. As a young man he was entirely at the mercy of Henry and that had curtailed many of his dreams and crushed most of his spirit. He wanted no such terrors for his own children and had let them have their heads freely.

He kissed his wife's overheated brow and made his way thoughtfully downstairs where he gathered his children to tell them Mama was poorly, but they had a new baby brother to welcome.

With typically childlike selfishness their sadness for Mama was fleeting, and the news of a new baby brother caused no excitement. Gabriel was still a baby and he was a spoilt misery

They clamoured to visit Mama's room but when told that she was sleeping they ran off happily, promptly forgetting her as they continued with their usual squabbling. The bigger ones racing ahead as Gabriel waddled behind them, squealing for them to wait for him

Hugh watched them with half an eye as he compiled a list of the things he must achieve the following day. If he could, he'd head off into town now to get things moving but he'd have to remain at home until the promised nurse came and that was all there was to it.

The following morning the nurse's arrival was felt in every corner of the house. She was a broad-hipped, formidable woman who took immediate control of the sickroom by throwing out the clutter that Gweneth loved and requesting a maid be sent up with cleaning materials.

She banished Matilda and the baby and requested that a small fold-out bed be placed at the foot of the bed in which her patient lay. She informed the entire household that she would rest when her patient rested and they were to be left entirely undisturbed.

This being the case she'd need complete freedom of the kitchens, her patient was to be encouraged to sleep as much as possible but, when awake would need simple, nourishing food which she, Nurse Barton, would prepare as required.

She ordered the fire in the bedroom to be lit and requested that a large supply of wood be made available as, regardless of the weather the windows were to remain wide open. Fresh air was what Mrs Daventor needed.

The cook was outraged, since her mistress had taken to her bed she'd come to enjoy her independence and resented this incomer and her new ways. She decided who ate what and when and she'd enjoyed ordering the maid about and was livid that a stranger had breezed in and was turning the accepted way of things upside down. She protested loudly but was quickly overruled.

The maid was sulky about the extra scrubbing she'd been forced to do, and the order that she was to present herself to the sickroom daily to do the same rankled. She was used to cook pushing her around, but she'd never expected her to do any scrubbing and she wouldn't be staying if this went on.

The footman complained about being asked to move beds from one room to another and shift chests up to the attic and fetch other stuff down but, as he'd been unkind to both the cook and the maid in the past, he got no sympathy from them.

Hugh breathed a sigh of relief and let Nurse Barton have her way. This left him to concentrate on the issue of childcare, which he was itching to do, he needed to get back to work.

Worcester Bridge Act - Notice is hereby given that a Meeting of the Trustees will be held at the Guildhall on Monday next at Ten-o-clock for the purpose of appointing Two-Toll-Gate-Keepers, one to collect the Toll on Foot Passengers, and the other to collect the Toll upon Horses, Cattle and carriages, by virtue of the new Act. By order of the Trustees, Michael Brown, Clerk. (Copyright and courtesy of the Worcester News)

CHAPTER THIRTY-FOUR

Ruby wasted no time telling Hugh he was asking for the impossible. 'No-one will take on a new-born child and five others below the age of ten.'

'Arthur is eleven.'

She smiled thinly. 'You need two people. A decent, motherly type to nurse the baby and oversee the basics of food and care for the others, all the things that their Mama is unable to do.'

He could see where she was going and nodded. 'And another to keep them out of trouble, a tutor maybe?'

'I can help you find the right woman, but I'll need to know where your home is to be? You mentioned Bransford?'

He shook his head sadly. 'Ah yes, Bransford was her dream. She wanted to get the children away from the canals and the tannery, had visions of a more genteel lifestyle for them. I went along with it, but to tell you the truth I don't want them to be genteel and spoilt and to look down on those who work for them. I've always been uncomfortable with that attitude.

'I couldn't move her now in any case, she's so frail.' He exhaled deeply, his sadness clear. 'I must be close to work so Bransford is an abandoned project.'

Ruby squeezed his arm and said gently, 'I wasn't asking you to explain yourself, but I need to know where to tell the girl she'll be working.'

He coloured up and shook his head apologetically. 'Her work will be in St Johns.'

'Good, St Johns is more convenient than Bransford. You do realise that *all* my girls have a past though? I don't want there to be any misunderstanding between us.'

'I know, and I trust your judgement. If you have someone in mind, then she'll have the position. Her past is neither here nor there as far as I'm concerned. I want my children to be properly cared for.'

The conversation ground to a halt when Eliza burst into the room shrieking for Ruby at the top of her voice. She liked things ordered and constantly made the mistake of asking the twins to help her when the urge to tidy up overtook her. Their refusal to support her resulted in tears and tantrums almost daily.

Georgie would not be pushed by anyone and a request or instruction usually resulted in her planting her hands on her hips and issuing a blunt no. She expected Emily to side with her, which she never failed to do. They would hold hands and skip away from their red-faced older sister leaving her feeling frustrated and lonely.

Ruby had expected that Eliza, the oldest and the most sensitive, to be a trial yet she found herself touched by the fact that whenever life did not go her way, the little girl looked to her for understanding, or explanations, and no-one else would do. Today being a case in point.

Once Juliet had come along and retrieved her charges, Hugh and Ruby shared a rueful glance. A house of children was never at peace.

'Juliet is as good as they come, and you can see my three are more than a match for her. You'll need quite a woman to cope with a half dozen. You do see that?'

'I do. We've allowed ours run a little wild, but I know that it's time to straighten them out, a tutor will be just the thing.'

'I can't help you there.'

He waved her concern away. 'There are any number of men currently offering themselves as tutors, I'll have no trouble finding the right one. How wonderful if I could find someone like our Sam.'

'A second Sam?' Ruby smiled. 'I wish you luck finding him.'

'I can't waste time getting help, the boys pair up and have endless fun, but I worry about Alice, she's often left out, being the only girl and I know she feels it badly.'

'Eliza is the same, we must see to it that they can spend time together, it will be good for them both. You do know Gweneth won't be happy to have one of my girls in her home?'

Hugh looked at the floor as he thought about his response. 'You're right, and I'm sorry for that. But she's not expected to recover you see. I need your help, not just now but later when…'

The silence sat heavily. Ruby hadn't realised the severity of the situation.

'I want someone kind but firm, I need to know that my children will be cherished and treated kindly when I'm not there. The woman you recommend will be secure as long as the welfare of my children is her priority.'

Ruby nodded her head once sharply. 'I'll send you her details as soon as I have her agreement.'

Satisfied and grateful, Hugh left Ruby and set off to begin his search for a tutor.

We state the following as a caution to those who are in the habit of riding their horses along public roads in a furious manner. An inquest was held last week at Inkberrow into the death of a woman who was rode over and killed on the spot by a man who, it appeared, was constantly riding furiously along the roads.

The coroner ordered the horse to be forfeited to the Lord of the Manor and the offender to pay all expenses incurred.

(Copyright and courtesy of the Worcester News)

CHAPTER THIRTY-FIVE

The news of Nelson's death travelled across the land in the wake of appropriately filthy weather. He'd lost his life in October and by December no-one spoke of much else. The Battle of Trafalgar was won but as King George said, *England has lost far more than she gained.*

Ruby considered herself fortunate to have been close enough to touch the great man once and she grieved for Emma Hamilton's loss as much as she did for her country.

Her thoughts turned to Richard who wrote rarely, and then only to confirm he was in no hurry to return to his old life. He'd found his place and was with the men he needed to be with. All that he owned he gave to her, to be held in trust for his daughters and he urged her to let the memory of him fade from their minds. He loved them and wanted the best for them, but fatherhood was not for him.

Her feelings for him were as confused as ever. She missed him and longed to see him, she was happy that he was at peace in his mind and she was furious that he'd walked away from his children.

'If he showed his face here tomorrow I'd bloody kill him.' She'd said after reading his latest letter.

Mary laughed. 'He knows that as well as anyone else. I doubt we'll see him until the girls are grown.'

It was all too sad now though. If a man like Nelson could lose his life, what chance had her boy to live a long life. So much fighting and so many deaths. The kindest thing was to stop speaking of him. If the girls asked about him she'd answer as best she could but otherwise, she'd do as he asked and allow the memory of him to slip away.

The funeral of Nelson occupied the country through the whole of January. As the funeral flotilla carried the fallen hero from Greenwich to Westminster, smaller but equally respectful flotilla travelled along every river in the land, saluted by canon and church bells.

Ruby cried as though she would never stop, and she really didn't know who she cried for.

You heard Trafalgar's story, you triumph in your country's glory,
mourn o'er the relics pale and gory, of Brave, Immortal Nelson.
To earth and War our Hero's dead, to Heaven and peace his spirit fled,
twine your green laurels around the head, of Brave, Immortal Nelson
(Copyright and courtesy of the Worcester News)

CHAPTER THIRTY-SIX

Sansome Springs in April was a glorious place to be and this year was better than most.

The numbers of visitors to the gardens increased, due to a combination of perfect weather and ongoing fascination with the new building that was only partially obscured by the screens.

The amount of bricks that had been seen wending their way by canal to the pleasure gardens had caused considerable speculation and that had simply increased month by month as other supplies were delivered.

There were rumours of great panes of glass being hoisted into place and people reported seeing tables and chairs being unloaded, so heavy that it took four men to lift a table. A vast sculpture of a woman was reported to be seen held aloft by a dozen men, so great was its size!

Francis Williams reaped the benefits of the mystery, people who had seen what was going on wanted to talk about having a small glass covered addition made to their own home or shop and his trade was booming.

The grand unveiling was scheduled and Barnabus was ready. The building work had taken much longer than he'd originally planned, but he'd learned from Ruby that you do it once and you do it right. Anything else cost too much, in terms of material, manpower and most of all, reputation.

This design had been so well thought out, and endlessly debated over, it should never need to be altered and would always prove adequate for the needs of Worcester.

The ladies would love the furniture, tables and chairs so heavy they couldn't be moved by one person and yet so skilfully crafted they appeared as delicate as lace. He agreed to furnish the name of the maker to anyone interested, for a small consideration.

The statue that had been sighted was a kneeling cherub with outstretched hands and was now situated at the far end of the pool in front of a pumping device which would cause spring water to trickle from her hands into the pool below. It was yet to be tested but there was time enough for any changes that may be required.

He'd kept Ruby up to date, withholding one secret, something he thought the most spectacular thing about the Spa. He planned to unveil it tomorrow when Ruby came to visit. He had a team of men rehearsing a demonstration again and again until they could do it blindfold.

Building the Spa had been reasonably problem free and it was almost at the end of the works that he had one heart stopping moment. The news of Nelson's death had plunged the country into mourning and every public place had commissioned a tribute. He knew he'd have to do likewise but how could he honour the man, and his war, adequately in a place devoted to the pleasure of women?

He agonised for days and it was Dennis who came to his rescue.

Just last month, amid much laughter and ribald jokes from his team of workers, a life-size painting of Lord Nelson and Emma Hamilton, walking hand in hand beside the water at Sansome Springs was hung in the entrance hall.

The great advantages of bathing, as well as preserving and restoring health, are widely evident to the public and, there appearing to be a deficiency of baths in this part of the country, Mr Stevenson most respectfully makes it known to the professional gentlemen of the neighbourhood that he intends to open an establishment of baths in Foregate Street. The facilities will include a vapour bath impregnated with the aroma of medicinal plants, a warm bath, a cold shower bath, a warm douche with a forcible stream of water, a slipper bath and a bath that can be prepared at any temperature. The charge will be £1 a quarter. The prime aim is to replicate the benefits offered by the most celebrated baths in Europe. (Copyright and courtesy of the Worcester News)

CHAPTER THIRTY-SEVEN

Barnabus's request that Ruby arrive at precisely two pm amused rather than irritated her. She'd learned a great deal in recent months, the most important of which was to trust those who'd never let her down. If he wanted to surprise her, then so be it.

She planned to make a day of it, bringing Mary, Bella, and the children with her. The Spa was her greatest investment to date and she wanted those she loved most to share the moment with her.

The girls had adapted well to their new lives, accepting Mary and Bella as part of their family with few questions.

Mary cooked and cared for the girls, treating them as though they were untrained puppies, well-loved but frequently annoying.

Bella, notoriously uncomfortable around children, tolerated them because they were Ruby's, and treated them as small adults and they adored her.

Juliet, who fought a daily battle against all the odds to turn them into ladies, had been given a much-needed day off.

Barnabus stood at the main gates, ready to greet her, his pride in his achievement heart-warming. She followed him along winding pathways that replaced the army of workers and mountains of rubble she'd become used to. Decorative screens were spread across the landscape, filling in gaps until the new planting filled out.

'We can still guarantee privacy you see.' He explained.

An elaborate gate was set into the hedging and it was only once through this that the Spa could be seen in all its glory. She paused her and drank in the sight.

Brick pillars, with glass doors set between them encircled a vast area. Great iron arches swooped from the tops of these pillars and panels of glass connected them like a fantastic spider's web.

'This is the only entrance,' he said. 'Once all the planting is at full strength this will become a secluded hideaway.'

Ruby's impatience overtook her. 'It's breath-taking. That glass, with the sun above and the water below, is wonderful. Let's go in, I've waited so long and I'm anxious to see it from the inside.'

Mary heard this and spoke out. 'You go on in Ruby, we'll stay out here with the girls.'

The children happily agreed. Mary let them make a noise and run around and there was always a chance that Bella would do something shocking if Ruby wasn't around to see.

Ruby stepped through the glass doors and stopped dead. She could instantly visualize the interior filled with women, taking tea, playing cards and sharing secrets with no men to disapprove or children to distract them. 'What a sanctuary you've designed, I feel like I'm dreaming.'

She wandered between the delicate tables and chairs, occasionally sitting in one and considering the room from that perspective, then moving on. 'I love the way you've created a feeling of intimacy here, despite the size of the place. So clever.'

She approached the stage at the far end and stood where a musician in the future might stand.

'Look to the far end of the pool.' Barnabus suggested.

She turned, and the pump gurgled into life, sending water gently through the cherub's fingers and into the pool below.

Ruby clapped her hands in excitement. 'I love it and you'll be rewarded, I promise you.'

'Let me show you the surprise, you knew about all of this.'

She nodded. 'You've made it so much more appealing than I'd imagined it though. You have an eye, and the passion to see it through to the end. Make no mistake I could not have built this miracle. You can see things I can't.'

He flushed bright red and stammered out his request for her to take a seat. He clapped his hands twice and his team of men stepped into place.

Water stopped flowing from the cherub's hands and a previously unnoticed door at the front of the stage slid open. Men removed a series of metal poles and rolled them into position across the top of the pool, forming a cage like covering.

Ruby stood up to get a better view.

The men carried out polished wooden boards and placed these on top of the cage. Once the final board was in place, they left.

'It's a ballroom, above a pool of water,' she gasped in amazement.

He nodded his head. 'It's a ballroom, a tea room, it's anything we wish. And that floor can be put into place in around half an hour and removed as quickly. We can have our Spa afternoons for ladies as planned, they'll be popular most of the year round, but we can do other things in the same space and the weather will make no difference.'

Ruby looked at him in admiration. 'This is beyond my imagining and I truly thank you.'

He laughed when she stepped gingerly onto the boards covering the pool. 'It's strong Ruby, we've tested it. The bars are made of the same material as the chairs and tables.'

'It's amazing and wonderful but how did you think of it, we never discussed anything like this?'

'It came up one day when I was speaking with Dennis and Josiah, the man that made the tables and chairs. He said it would be simple to do if we made it to measure from the start. That's why we needed a step down into the pool, it allows the floor to be flush with the surrounding area. Without that extra step this floor would be raised and that wouldn't work if we wanted to hold a ball in here.'

His chest puffed with pride, he'd been sure she'd approve but one should never take Ruby for granted.

'It's spectacular, far better than I had hoped. The cost has been colossal, but we've got so much more than I had bargained for. I look forward to hearing your plans of filling this up with people, I'm certain you've had some thoughts.'

'I've devoted as much thought as I could to it and every day it seems something else occurs to me. I think I've had so much to think about that I may have driven myself a little mad. I know we must open this up to the city formally but I'm going to need to talk to you about that.'

She nodded her understanding. 'Then take some time for yourself, rest and clear your mind, I don't need anything more from you. I want you to be well and strong for the summer ahead. I'll ponder an opening ceremony and we'll talk frequently in the meantime.'

After checking that he needed nothing more from her, she left him to enjoy his Spa.

She found Mary on her back, face to the sun and happily ignoring the children. Ruby gathered them up, insisting they see the Spa from the inside. The girls immediately started playing chase through the open doors, while Mary gazed about open mouthed as the earlier performance was now played out in reverse, the polished floor being replaced by a shining blue pool.

'Bloody hell Ruby, he's a marvel, that fellow of yours.'

Ruby nodded happily. 'That he is. Come on, let's get out of his way now you've seen it. I need a stretch.'

She led them all around her pleasure gardens. The girls were bored at the archery butts but entranced by Battledore and Shuttlecock. When they tired of this distraction, which was long after Ruby tired of it, she showed them where Bowls and Ninepins were played.

Ruby and Bella joined the game and a fierce competition was fought, aided by Mary, randomly calling out encouragement to whoever's name she could remember.

It was a very lively group that eventually found themselves at the labyrinth, Ben's pride and joy. He'd done an incredible job, laying the pathway first with red and green tiles and then edged it with slow growing scented shrubs.

Ruby explained what Ben had said. 'The point of a labyrinth is to walk slowly and simply enjoy the serenity. Don't think or plan and don't wait for the destination, just relax.'

Mary and Bella looked blankly at her and she laughed and suggested it was time to go home.

Last night, a new equestrian school opened for the first time in the Tything, adjoining this city, with a company of performers, which has never been equalled before a Worcester audience, for ability in their different departments. The boxes were genteelly filled, and from the manifest applause they incessantly bestowed on the elegant performances of the Young Saunders, and the admiration with which they beheld the astonishing athletic powers of Mr Ireland, together with their approbation of the general abilities of the company, promises that during their visit, the proprietors will meet with adequate encouragement for the expenses they have incurred in erecting such an elegant temporary and selected accommodation for public amusement. (Copyright and courtesy of the Worcester News)

CHAPTER THIRTY-EIGHT

The doctor advised Hugh to send for the parson, saying he had another patient to visit but then he would return.

Gweneth hadn't left her bed since Nathaniel's traumatic birth fourteen months ago. The children had almost forgotten what it was like to have a happy and healthy Mama. Nathaniel had never known his mother and was barely aware of what was happening.

Hugh felt the loss keenly, he'd been full of hope and expectation when he and Gweneth had married. She'd been exactly what he needed. An absolute tower of strength when he was at his lowest point who'd gone on to give him six wonderful children whilst building a secure home for them all.

He'd spent years making his own way in the world and had become roughened, she helped him find a middle ground, not perfect, but something they both could live with. And now she was leaving him.

He hoped that she'd known how much he'd loved her and how important she'd been to him. He'd done his best to ensure her last months were as pain free as possible and he was grateful that their children had been able to get used to living without her slowly.

He was thankful that both of her parents were dead and would not need to suffer the pain of her passing. That burden would be his alone.

At the urging of the parson he brought the children up to say goodbye. Gabriel fought to get away from the sombre room and was handed over to Arthur, as Hugh held Nathaniel. Percival squealed when asked to kiss Mama whilst Alice, holding Freddie's hand, whispered goodbye. The parson read from the bible and they mumbled along with the prayer before Hugh let them go.

He took his wife's hand and prepared to sit with her until the end. With the first light of dawn Gweneth stopped breathing.

He went downstairs and gathered Freddie, Arthur and Alice, his oldest three and told them. 'I'm depending on you three bigger ones to help me with the others.' Their pride at being treated as grown-ups made him want to weep for them.

'You understand that Mama has been very poorly and is now at peace, she has no more pain.' They nodded solemnly, and he smiled at their sweet and trusting faces.

'I want you to promise me there'll be no foolish pranks played for the time being. Lots of people will be coming to see us in the next few days and I want you to make me proud of you.'

He spoke seriously. 'You must help me to keep the little ones quiet and away from Mama's room. Can you do that?'

All three nodded. 'I knew I could depend on you.' He gave Alice a kiss on the cheek and ruffled the boys' hair. 'You're all so grown up now,'

There was no more to say, Hugh watched as they finished their supper and made their preparations for bed with not a tantrum or a sulk between them. He was sad for that.

*On Sunday morning the lifeless corpse of a young
woman was found by the side of the Worcester and
Bromyard Road near Bringsty. It is supposed that being
unwell or tired, she sat down and became so numbed
from the extreme cold that she was unable to walk on
and consequently perished.
(Copyright and courtesy of the Worcester News)*

CHAPTER THIRTY-NINE

Bella ran as fast as she could through The Foregate and used the last of her strength to hammer on Ruby's front door, unaware that it was barely six am.

Mary flung open the door, angrily muttering at such a racket being raised before decent folk had breakfasted. She was pushed back into the hallway by Bella who thrust a bundle of papers at her.

'Here, read this while I catch my breath.' She managed to gasp.

Ruby came running down the stairs and took the bundle as Mary helped Bella to a chair and poured her a drink.

One of the papers was half a page torn from a London newspaper and told the tale of Mathuselah Spalding who had recently been hanged in that city, after being found guilty of committing an unnatural crime with another man. The other sheet was a scrap of different paper, it was soiled and smeared and had handwritten words scrawled across it. The writing was poor and smudged but Ruby could make out a few of the words.

...burn down your molly house...
...burned alive and...

Ruby passed the papers to Mary and put her arms around her old friend. 'How did you come by these pieces of filth?'

Bella, a lifelong source of laughter and strength sat, white faced and trembling. She sucked in a ragged breath. 'I was getting ready for bed last night when I heard a shout of fire. I ran across the lane and saw flames coming from the stables, we all set to and put it out. It wasn't too bad, not like it could have been. The horses were spooked but not hurt and we were all safe in a couple of hours.'

She paused to gulp gratefully at the drink Mary had put in her hand. 'The late ones went off home then and we all went to our beds. This morning that daft Toby comes running into my place crying and carrying on, he'd found them papers pushed under their door when he got up in the night.'

Mary moaned quietly. 'The fire was set deliberately? Who would do such a thing?'

The three women looked at each other in horror. Fire was a danger that they all lived with and it was sickening to imagine the evil it took to set light to a home.

'We have to report this Bella, and you should shut up shop. It's not safe for you to carry on with wicked bastards like this running about.'

'It's wicked all right but there's not a chance of me closing. It's upset all the fellows and some of them don't want to stay, but there's a few like me who won't be told what we can do. I'll stay and fight until I've no breath left rather than run scared. I'll tell you that.'

'Close up for a few days while this can be looked into at least. You know there's an army of folks who want places like yours shut down, why don't you think about it? Attitudes are changing.'

Bella laughed at this. Her colour had returned to normal and now she'd worked out a lot of her temper on her walk she was feeling better. 'You've forgotten all you ever knew if you think that. I won't be chased off and that's that.'

Ruby had a nasty feeling the threat was serious and she shuddered to think of harm coming to warm hearted Bella. 'Give it up. Come and stay here with us, you don't need to be doing it anymore.'

Bella shook her head stubbornly. 'I'm not going to start drinking tea and dressing like a lady. I like my life just fine, and anyhow, you don't want those girls of yours to have too much contact with me. I might lead them astray.'

'This is serious Bella.'

'It is. But now I've calmed down I reckon it was some poor sod who hasn't got the stomach to face what's wrong in his own life, so he'll take a shot at mine. But those houses are mine and I won't be run off.'

'I know how you feel but you've only got to read that newspaper to see that folks today can't bear to hear about anyone who lives a bit different to them or having something they're not having. They'd sooner hang them than let them live in peace. It's not right but you should take this seriously before real trouble comes to your door.'

Bella shook her head. 'It's a cruel world Ruby, I'll tell you that. Those boys of mine are as happy and gentle as could be and how anyone could threaten to burn them alive is beyond me.'

Bella had been in the business of selling sex all her life and despite being reviled for it, had never knowingly hurt another person. She spread joy and laughter to all who got to know her and the thought of her being in danger made Ruby shiver.

She dropped to her knees and clasped Bella's hands. 'I understand, I'm a fighter too, you know that, but you don't know who you're fighting, and you can't tell how serious they are. Give it up Bella, you don't need the money.'

'And turn my boys and girls out? What would become of them? They've got nothing apart from me. Those houses were there for us when we had nowhere to go and I feel obliged to keep them going for others now.'

Ruby knew when she was beaten. 'Let's set up a watch then, I'll find a few fellows to keep an eye out for anyone acting strange nearby.'

At this Bella wiped her tears and let out a bellow of laughter. 'You know as well as I do that everyone who comes to my place is acting strange, that's my speciality. Guards would frighten them all off. Report it if you must but there's to be no watch kept outside my house.'

There was no point in arguing, what she'd said was true, her business would wither if guards were posted outside. Ruby would report the attack and hand over the papers that had been found but she'd continue to urge Bella to give up her business.

Her friend had been out there for so long she hadn't realised that there was an unpleasant mood sweeping the country.

People still wanted their dirty secrets, but there was nothing secret about Bella's bawdy houses.

On Wednesday night about 11 o'clock, a fire was discovered in the china manufactory of Messrs Grainger, Wood and Co., situated in Lowesmoor, Worcester. On the alarm being given, the neighbours and inhabitants gave the most active assistance. The flames were got under control by about 2 o'clock in the morning. The building, with various valuable articles contained in it, was entirely consumed.
(Copyright and courtesy of the Worcester News)

CHAPTER FORTY

Hannah almost skipped up the stairs to the re-furbished apartments that were her own. She smiled with pleasure at first sight of the haven that Francis Williams had created for her, even though it had been completed a year ago. He'd transformed the space and changed her life. She was better rested and in a far happier frame of mind, she felt appreciated and cherished and she approached every day with a renewed sense of optimism.

At the top of the stairs was a light and open room that had been furnished with soft, warm chairs and glossy wooden furniture. There were books on the shelves and pretty drapery at the windows. A large round table in the centre of the room was where Hannah and her two assistants spent most of their leisure time. Here they played cards, sewed and chattered about the business of the day.

At each end of this room were two small bedrooms. Louisa and Polly, her new assistants, took one end and Hannah the other.

Hannah missed her friendship with Ellie, but there was no doubt her new role as guide and teacher was deeply satisfying. The girls injected fun and laughter into what had become routine work. They were hard working, ambitious and thrilled to have been given this opportunity.

Louisa was a jolly larger-than-life girl who was never without a smile. The modern trend was for a tiny waist on a girl, but Louisa was happy with herself the way God made her, with big breasts and a thick waist, she was strong, and she liked that. Her curly, chestnut brown hair glowed like satin and her creamy complexion owed nothing to the arts she practised. She approached life with a smile and a warm heart, liking everyone she met and assuming she was liked back. She looked for happiness every day and always found it.

Polly was tall and thin, with silvery hair and pale eyes. She was inclined to be reserved, not being as generous in her thoughts and attitudes as the other girl. However, it was impossible to hold onto reserve around Louisa and Polly soon stopped trying and became a loyal shadow and partner.

In the beginning the two younger women had hung on to Hannah's every word. They paid close attention to her teaching and were the best of students, Polly was a quick learner needing to be shown a process only once before being able to replicate it.

Louisa required time and practice, but she would often be the one to say, *I wonder what would happen if...?* She loved to experiment and was always willing to submit her own skin and hair to test something even as the other two urged caution.

As their confidence grew they questioned some things Hannah taught them and this prompted her to consider adopting a different approach. She'd been doing what she did for so long that she'd stopped experimenting and these two determined young women reminded her that new products and solutions were always needed.

The new products gained better results and tempted new clients. Madame Eloise was once again all the rage.

Hannah and Ellie continued to meet weekly, but their visits were awkwardly formal.

Ellie felt humiliated that Hannah knew more about her marital woes than an outsider should, and she hated that she'd been brought so low in front of another woman.

Hannah's burden was in knowing that Ellie had endured misery and her carefree happiness was gone, maybe forever. She sensed a deep unhappiness in the household and wondered if she should raise her concerns with Ruby.

The sisters met regularly, and Hannah hated to interfere. She already knew more about the two intensely private women that any of them would choose. Why risk making future relations more strained? She cared deeply for them both. Surely all they wanted now was her discretion.

Mrs Painter, late professor of music in London,
respectfully informs the nobility and gentry of Worcester
and its environs that she instructs ladies in the piano
forte, singing, harp, lute and guitar at the residence of
the pupil or at her own.
(Copyright and courtesy of the Worcester News)

CHAPTER FORTY-ONE

At the first hint of fire, the nearest church bells would ring out and the men that managed the cumbersome fire wagon, two horses, a pump and a tough of water, would head in that direction. At the same time, two small boys scampered through the tracks and alleys to identify the actual building on fire. It was a slow and inaccurate procedure.

Ruby heard the alarming church bells away in the distance, the pain of losing Tom spiked from a constant ache she could control, to a sharp stab that stole her breath. She gripped the back of the chair and bent in to the agony. Tom dead, Richard estranged, Baby Thomas gone, Elizabeth, Ma. If not for the girls…

The door to the small dining room burst open and her ugly thoughts were pushed to the background by excited giggles and tale telling.

Juliet's plea to remember they were young ladies and not wild animals brought a smile to her face. Their antics and naughtiness were a daily source of happiness. She was better at this second attempt at motherhood.

Juliet's resolve to turn her girls into ladies was admirable and amusing in view of their family background but she was resolute, working on the assumption that if a thing is ignored, it ceases to be.

Ruby knew that no pig's ear was ever turned into a silk purse and doubted they'd reach middle society with her blood running in their veins, however, with confidence and pep, they'd do well enough for all that.

'Girls! Sit down now or there'll be no breakfast for you.' Juliet battled on.

They heard the bells of the fire wagon as it approached and ran screaming to the window to watch as the cumbersome apparatus was hauled past, slopping precious water from side to side and soaking the walkways.

The door burst open and a voice shouted, 'Ma Jebb's is on fire.'

Ruby stood up so fast her chair clattered on the floor behind her.

'I've sent a note to the Hop Pole and a cart is on its way to collect you.' The maid said, knowing that Ruby would need to go.

'Bless you Sally.' Mary said, as she came running.

Ruby was too concerned about Bella to have even heard the girl. She reached the front door at the same time as the promised cart and both women climbed aboard and urged the groom to make haste.

They could smell the fire before they could see it and instinctively they gripped the other's hand tightly. The roof of the main house had fallen in entirely as had one of the long walls that ran parallel to the road. The once secretive and forbidden interior pathetically exposed to the gawping eyes of those who had come out to see the sight.

The smaller house still stood, but its roof was ablaze sending up the thick, black smoke they'd seen from their cart. The little building trembled before their eyes and with a growl, collapsed in on itself, spewing out a cloud of dust that blinded everyone and set them all coughing.

Ruby screamed out for Bella as she headed toward the inferno, only stopping when Mary grabbed her around the waist.

She fought hard, but Mary clung on. 'You can't see nothing, wait until it settles.'

'Oh God, where is she.' Ruby howled in pain and screamed her friend's name. She'd ceased struggling but couldn't stop calling out desperately. Her eyes shone wildly through a coat of ash.

As the dust settled the outlines of people and buildings gradually became visible and they saw the shocking empty space where the smaller of the two houses had stood for more years than anyone there could remember. Now it was reduced to a pile of charred wood. The big house was still standing but it wouldn't stay that way for long.

Ruby shook herself free and her eyes raked the avid onlookers until she spotted a couple of faces she recognised in a sad little huddle some way apart from the main body of onlookers. She picked her way over to them as the eyes of the crowd followed her.

'Talking to them makes you as bad as them.' A woman called out, setting off a barrage of abuse that Ruby was deaf to.

Mary was a different matter, she turned furiously on the rabble. 'Jane Goode who goes to church every day and twice on Sunday, where's the God in your heart, you wicked bitch? And you, Tom Wilson, gloating over the destruction of a place that saw more of your money than your children ever did. You sicken me, the miserable fucking lot of you.' She tossed them a glance of disgust and moved to stand by Ruby as she questioned Bella's workers.

'She shouted out the alarm and I saw her a while ago, she kept going back in to bring others out.' Sobbed one of the young men. 'I didn't see her come out the last time.'

Ruby gripped his arm so tightly he winced. 'Where did you see her last. Show me exactly.'

'I'm not sure, I don't know.' He gabbled in his panic.

Ruby slapped him. 'She saved your life, now save hers. Where was she?'

He pointed. 'She went back into the big house, that was the last time I saw her.'

Ruby was off and running toward the collapsed wall of the big house.

A man reached out his arm to stop her, but she shook him off. 'I lived here all my life, I know this warren better than anyone, let me go.'

She picked her way over the glowing embers wincing as the heat burned her feet and screaming Bella's name as she vanished from view.

The officers mingled with the crowd and gathered names and as much information as they could but no-one, apart from Mary, followed Ruby towards the ruin.

The buildings were a source of shame and if anyone had friends out here, well they were a whore or a whore lover. Not worth risking a decent life for.

A terrifying scream echoed around the damaged buildings and Mary responded. 'I'm here Ruby, where are you?'

The crowd fell silent as a smoke blackened figure staggered into view, half carrying a body. A man stepped forward to help, then another. Ruby and the body of Bella were gently lifted away from the scorched remains and placed on the cart heading to the infirmary.

Ruby didn't feel the blistering on her hands or feet, her burning eyes and rasping throat were nothing. She'd been too late to prevent Bella's death and nothing else mattered. She cried for the loss of that beautiful and vibrant woman who laughed and loved her way through every day that God gave her.

She'd met Bella at the worst time in her life and Bella had managed to both shock and amuse her every day since. They'd been closer than sisters and she couldn't breathe through the agony of losing her.

A wretched emptiness swept through her and she howled out her anguish. Why Bella? The one person who would share anything she owned if it would help another out.

Sweet Bella, who didn't know how to refuse a call for help.

Some false and alarming reports having prevailed in relation to several incendiary papers which have lately appeared in this City of Worcester, we thought it necessary to publish a copy in order to dispel the terror with which the minds of some people seemed to be affected. Here is a copy of a paper stuck up against the door of Mr Stokes, glover in High Street. 'If you keep these theatrical players, by God you and your family shall suffer by God and by fire, so part with them and you shall be safe from damnation.'
(Copyright and courtesy of the Worcester News)

CHAPTER FORTY-TWO

Laughter rang out in the Pargeter home. An increasingly frequent event since Ellie had returned with her baby.

Harold had greeted her politely and had been welcoming to his sons, baby included, but had made himself scarce since then. He was still a presence of course, but the civil distance they maintained suited them both.

She chased the squealing boys around the upper floor of their home. Baby Mathew was easy, his chubby legs pumped furiously but he was left behind by his brothers, Sam and Si who, despite being much more grown up, were proud of their baby brother and always joined in the childish games of chase and hide-and-seek that he loved to play, allowing themselves to be found just a second before his bottom lip trembled.

He didn't understand the puzzles and tricks that amused them, but he laughed when they laughed and that gave him as much pride as if he'd understood the joke.

The church bells chimed out the hour and their laughter stopped abruptly. Without a word being spoken the small group made their way down to the middle floor. Sam and Si pulled out their work books and, after settling Mathew down to play at her feet with some wooden farm animals, Ellie picked up her sewing.

Harold entered the room, as anticipated. He tested the boys on the lessons he'd wanted them to work on and grunted his approval at their response. Ellie respected his pride in his sons and made sure they never disappointed him.

Satisfied that they'd done their work diligently he turned his attention to Ellie. 'How was your day? I trust Mathew was well behaved?'

'He was an angel, as ever. I'm very proud of our three boys.'

He inclined his head, showing he expected no less.

'Hugh will be joining us tomorrow for dinner dear, I hope your business will allow you an evening at home.' She said, stifling a smile. The only time he ever spent an evening at home was when Hugh visited.

Harold was resentfully certain that Hugh's patronage was paying dividends, he'd had a very good run in the shop and was most unlikely to forget a dinner date with him.

'I'm looking forward to it. Now, if you'll excuse me I'll bid you good night?' He nodded his head in her direction and left the room.

The boys studied their books and she continued with her sewing until the front door slammed.

Sam tiptoed across the room and peered through the window. Turning back to the room he plucked a ball of paper from his pocket and threw it at Si, a signal that they were free to be themselves again.

*A beautiful meteor was observed from this City on
Monday night at half past ten. It shot across the heavens
with the appearance of a blue flame and luminous ring,
in which state it was for some time visible.
(Copyright and courtesy of the Worcester News)*

CHAPTER FORTY-THREE

It was confirmed that the fire that killed Bella had been set deliberately.

Everyone knew what used to go on out at the old houses and although many respectable people disapproved of the business, burning folk in their beds was not the answer.

The parish officers questioned locals, certain that someone knew something about the events of that day and hoping the collective conscience of the city would force them to hand the information over.

Ruby ignored everything in the month following Bella's death. Uninterested in anything but her own loss. Nothing penetrated the shell she'd managed to crawl behind, not the girls, not Mary, and not Ellie. They all tried and were all defeated, though they persisted.

'I should have made her give it up Mary. I can't bear to think that she died through something I gave her.' She cried piteously one night.

'She died because some wicked bastard did a cowardly thing. It was nothing to do with you and you must stop blaming yourself.

'Be thankful for the happy times we shared. Years and years of laughing and secrets, don't let anything overshadow all that joy. Don't put dark clouds where there were none. We made the best out of the life we were given and all three of us were better for having each other.'

'It's too much Mary, how much more must I lose?'

'I wish I could say there'll be no more, but that's not possible. I'm here and will be for as long as I breathe, but where's the fighter that I know and love? I can't watch you give up. It's time to look to your girls, they need you.'

Ruby drained her glass and re-filled it, turning her body away from Mary, who sighed sadly and left her alone.

The plans for the grand opening of the Spa that Ruby had been so particular about were cancelled. She had no interest in the Spa or the gardens and had forbidden any event.

Instead she spent hours raging at the fire wagon that stood by because Bella wasn't insured by them.

She railed against a God who'd robbed her time and again. Of her innocence, of her sons and grandson, and now of her dearest friend. She couldn't reconcile in her mind how anyone could light a fire designed to burn innocent folk as they slept, yet the evidence showed that this was indeed what had occurred.

'Why?' She'd cry.

The newspapers almost gloried in the lurid story hinted at in the papers Bella had found. A group of men were charged with having unnatural relationships with other men.

The stories promoted an upsurge in rigid minded souls who felt it was their duty to clean the world. The colourful reporting had many people convinced that a plague of perversion was spreading across the land and must be stopped in its tracks.

The evidence began to point to one man, a travelling preacher, who'd walked the villages of

Worcestershire for as long as anyone could recall, preaching the word of God and threatening all manner of hell and damnation to sinners.

As a younger man he had been tolerated, even welcomed, he was lively and clever, and he spoke of things that people wanted to believe in. He'd read bible stories and lead hymn singing, he'd answer their questions and, in return was given food, clothing and a place to sleep.

The years had not been kind to Journeyman Jesus however. He'd become a ranting hysteric, a filthy man who slept where he fell and was liked by no-one. He travelled from town to village spouting his own interpretation of the bible but had few listeners. His views had narrowed, and he'd been known to call for cleansing by fire.

It was years before people realised that it was he who stole from them, it was he who threatened their children with his stick and, in view of all that, it was probably he who had killed the young maid that had been found dead in a ditch a couple of years ago.

Evidence of his guilt came when the ruins had cooled, and a huge book was uncovered in the search. The covers and edges of the bible were scorched and curled, yet it was still recognisable when found near a door that had fallen. His charred body was weighted down by the same door.

Ruby wasn't interested. 'Knowing who the mad bastard was won't bring her back, will it?' She shouted at Mary who had delivered the information.

'No, but at least we know he'll never hurt another poor soul.'

'Pah.' Ruby shook her head in disgust.

Mary feared she'd lost Ruby as well as Bella. She'd always been strong and certain, and it broke her heart to see her so diminished.

It was also terrifying because her people looked to Mary, in the absence of Ruby, for answers and she found herself dealing with matters she neither knew or cared about. She lay awake at nights wondering what she was doing and who she was meant to turn too.

Everyone needed advice or support occasionally, but Ruby had given up.

The Parish officer of Broadwas has apprehended an idle, disorderly vagabond person that could give no account of himself. And in his custody was found a silver chalice, supposed to be part of some church plate, and also a silver spoon. Whatever person or parish has lost the above mentioned things should apply themselves to Rowland Bartley Esq of Cotheridge, and proving it is their due, may have the said plate restored.
(Copyright and courtesy of the Worcester News)

CHAPTER FORTY-FOUR

Barnabus channelled his energy and ingenuity into planning a grand opening for Sansome Spa, despite being forbidden to do any such thing.

To his mind, too much time and money had been invested in the project for him to do anything but launch the thing properly. Ruby was not in her right mind and, as her business manager, it was his duty to protect her from her own neglect.

He'd thought long and hard about the issue. The opening had to be big and bold and showy, he needed to draw a crowd and he had to send them home with something to talk about. But he had to be respectful in view of Ruby's personal sadness.

The scheduled opening date of August had long since passed, he'd had to work far harder than Ruby might have have needed to, but he'd given it his all, and everything had come together. And now the moment of truth had arrived. The October day dawned bright and clear and he gave thanks for that.

Ruby's friends had rallied with help and advice and he was nervous but optimistic. Those closest to Ruby assured him that she'd have heard that there was an event planned - it was the talk of the town after all - and they believed she was allowing it to go ahead because it was the right thing to do.

His gut had churned for weeks, and his palms were constantly damp with sweat, but when his nerves threatened to get the better of him, he reminded himself this was his job. It was what she paid him to do.

He'd worked himself to a standstill with this and expected the staff to match his efforts. Every pane of glass had been buffed and polished, inside and out, until the reflection of the water flashed and sparkled across the gardens like a beacon in the early morning light.

Every little swoop and swirl of the fancy ironwork had been wiped free of dust and the plants in their tubs glowed greenly. The cherub with the trickling water was primed and ready to impress.

A glossy piano was set, glowing richly in the centre of the stage, and every one of the tables was placed exactly so. The glass doors were wide open allowing the music to be heard for some distance.

The opening had been advertised for mid-morning and his intention was to give small groups a guided tour of the new addition and then have them lured away to head on up to other attractions, leaving the Spa clear for the next small group to enjoy.

Throughout his planning he'd constantly reflected on all Ruby had taught him. She may have forbidden this launch, but he'd make damned sure she wouldn't be embarrassed by it.

Great braziers lined the walkways and between them sat vats of hot spiced wine, to be dispensed freely. Every door in every building was to be left wide open from midday, should the weather turn nasty, he wanted people to find shelter and be encouraged to stay.

At the appointed hour Dennis gave the agreed signal and the pianist began to play as the cherub with her water added a glorious accompaniment and the first group of people approached.

The next group would follow in thirty minutes, it was important that people saw and appreciated the Spa in small groups but then that they be moved on to allow others to do the same. The men on the gate were responsible for keeping to that plan.

Lillian had the task of moving the first crowd onwards, once the next group approached.

The sighs of amazement and the bubble of chatter that burst forth from the first visitors reassured them all and Barnabus began his rehearsed announcement confidently.

'Our Spa will be open to ladies, every afternoon, from tomorrow. We'll serve refreshments, and ladies may bathe or simply sit here and enjoy the fresh air in peace and tranquillity.'

'What, are no men allowed entry?' Asked a deep voice from the back of the crowd.

Barnabus smiled as he shook his head.

'Afternoons are reserved for females only. However, we'll be holding a monthly ball here, to which you're all invited.'

'A ball, in a pool. Are you mad?' The man called as laughter erupted.

Barnabus smiled as his men moved in and began to lay the wooden boards over the water and the laughter ceased. A couple of fellows bounced up and down, to test it, and the group was ushered out, to make room for the next.

The day continued in this fashion, a few stragglers from each group refused to be moved on and the tables gradually filled up. He'd expected this and appreciated that the little rounds of applause he received after each introduction grew louder and longer. As the afternoon wore on, the volume of visitors slowed and the need to funnel them onwards was over.

At around three pm a carefully orchestrated commotion attracted startled glances and drew groups of people towards the unseen source. Others followed and as they reached the brow of a hill there were cries of delight, here was the spectacle they'd been promised.

Two brothers had come to demonstrate their air balloon, sight few expected to witness. Excitement crackled through the crowd and, just like water trickling from the hands of the cherub, they flowed downhill to listen to the young men speak about their passion.

The audience marvelled at the massive basket attached to the mounds of fabric strewn across the gardens. The sheer weight made them doubt that it would float above their heads. As the brothers spoke, the balloon began to fill up, and the basket suddenly didn't look so big.

'Wouldn't get me in it, that's for sure.'

'I should hope not, the size of your guts would weight the bugger down for sure.'

What had appeared ungainly was transformed into a thing of grace and beauty. The gold and white balloon trembled then listed, first one way, then the other, causing gasps of fear to ripple through the crowd.

The two men jumped into the basket as it soared gently upwards.

The crowd roared in appreciation as it rose higher and was off, following the curves of the river.

Ruby, alone in her orchard, watched with clenched fists and fixed jaw as the balloon floated overhead, twisting in the breeze and exposing the golden letters on the side that spelled out the name of her friend. Bella.

The heat of the weather for the last few days in and around Worcester has been as great as it usually is in the hottest months. The weather has in consequence been very tempestuous and on Monday the lightening was uncommonly vivid and accompanied by awful peals of thunder.

(Copyright and courtesy of the Worcester News)

CHAPTER FORTY-FIVE

Hannah felt, rather than heard, a muffled thumping that had her up and on her feet in seconds.

'It's coming from this wall.' Polly pointed in confusion.

'It's Ellie next door. Shout through and tell her I'm coming.' Hannah called as she flew down the stairs and out into the street to hammer on the door, Louisa close behind her.

One of the boys let them in, a break in his voice betraying him. 'Pa's unwell and we can't wake him.' He pointed upstairs.

Hannah started to climb. 'I'm here Ellie.' She shouted. 'Where are you?'

She followed Ellie's voice and found her sitting on the floor beside Harold, who was flat on his back.

'I heard him scream and I ran to help, but I'm afraid he's dead.'

The boy stood by the door looking terrified.

Hannah turned to Louisa, 'Take him out and run to the infirmary for help. Quickly now.'

He turned to Ellie, fear in his eyes, she mustered a smile and nodded. 'Go on now.'

'I shouldn't have let him see, but I didn't know what had happened until too late.' She sobbed into Hannah's shoulder.

'Don't worry about that now. Where's Matthew?' Hannah could see Harold was beyond help.

'He's asleep, upstairs.'

'I'll look after him.' Polly said, arriving in time to hear her.

A doctor came and pronounced Harold dead. He examined the contents of the room, pulling out drawers and opening cupboards until at last he found something that caused him to grunt in satisfaction.

'Damn fool thing to do, keeping sulphuric acid about the place, it should be kept under lock and key.' He held the bottle up for them to see and shook his head in disbelief that an intelligent man could behave in such a reckless manner.

The magistrate was informed, and then the coroner. In due course the death was pronounced a dreadful accident.

It appeared Harold had drunk from a bottle containing sulphuric acid, mistaking it for a cough syrup he made for himself. He sold that very product in his shop as a treatment for foot rot in sheep and he was criticised for becoming careless with something he was so familiar with.

The coroner ordered an announcement to be placed in the newspapers urging all households to be vigilant when keeping poisons about the home.

Harold had made his wishes known and his paperwork was up to date. His house and business were left to Ellie and, upon her death, to his sons.

Last week an inquest was held in the parish of Hampton Lovett on the body of a fine boy, about a year and three-quarters old, whose death was occasioned by poison. It appeared that the deceased, with his two sisters under eight years of age, was at play in the parlour of their father's house where several phial bottles were standing in the window. One of them was forced from the window by the children and the deceased wanted to taste the contents. The elder sister, thinking it contained syrup, pulled out the cork and put the bottle to his lips. He drank some of the contents and instantly cried in great agony and, upon immediate examination of the bottle, its contents were found to be sulphuric acid or oil of vitriol, a deadly poison which had been used for curing foot rot in sheep. Verdict-Accidental Death.
(Copyright and courtesy of the Worcester News)

CHAPTER FORTY-SIX

The news of Harold's death reached Hugh, who felt only relief. His hands were more than full coping with his children and directing two new members of the household.

That he no longer needed to protect Ellie from her husband left him free to concentrate his attention on business and setting up his household for the future.

He imagined Ruby and Ellie would take care of each other and it was not until a desperate Barnabus called on him for help that he realised how mistaken he'd been.

'I apologise for disturbing you Sir, but I don't know what else to do. I hope I've done the right thing.'

He shuffled awkwardly and scraped his hair back with one hand and wiped the other on the leg of his trousers.

'Come in and catch your breath man. Did you run here? No, don't speak, I'll get you a drink while you calm down.'

Barnabus gratefully took the drink and reminded himself that Daventor was just a man, and a business man at that.

Hugh urged him to sit. 'Now then, tell me what brings you out here?'

Barnabus nodded. 'It's the Sansome Springs account, it's run dry and I have bills to pay. I know Ru… Miss Morgan, counts you as family. She'll kill me for betraying her, but if I don't pay up, the gardens will be at risk.'

'And you're talking to me because?'

'She won't see anyone, hasn't since Bella died.'

'I see. Everyone I know speaks highly of your new attraction, surely it's not failing?'

'No, it's a great success, but running costs are high, we expected it to take one, possibly two years for us to see a profit and we have plans in place, but we need Ruby's signature to release funds and nothing else will do.'

Hugh knew he must be a last resort. 'You've tried to speak to her I take it?'

'She's not seeing anyone. I've called on her a couple of times and left messages, but I can't get any response.'

Hugh nodded decisively. 'I'm glad you came to me, you've done the right thing. Refer all creditors to me, there'll be no more trouble for you from that quarter. Draw up a list and give it to Barker. He'll sort the finances out and I'll sort Ruby out. And don't worry, you've taken the only course open to you and she'll be grateful, I'll see to that.'

The two men shook hands and parted.

Hugh issued a flurry of instructions to his staff and the following morning saw him hammering impatiently on Ruby's front door.

Mary answered. 'I'm coming as fast as I can, hold your blasted horses.' She threw open the door and looked him up and down with a scowl of irritation. 'She's not seeing anyone, and I've got me bloody hands full, so be quick.'

He stepped in a cast his eyes around. 'Where is she, and where are the girls?

'The girls are upstairs running rings around Juliet, Ruby has a headache, and I'm at the end of my bleeding rope, so I'll thank *you* to speak to *me* with a bit of respect, unless you want to go prancing back to St Johns with a black eye.'

His eyes sparkled, and his lips twitched. 'I apologise for my abrupt manner. I'm here to help.'

She sniffed and, seeing he was determined, brought him up to date.

He ignored her flinch as he patted her arm. 'I'm going up to see her, headache or not, this nonsense has gone on long enough, do you agree?'

She shrugged but stepped back, allowing him room to reach the stairs. He took them two at a time and she followed. If he could pull off a miracle then she'd like to see it.

He paused at the top of the stairs and, after glancing at Mary for a sign that he'd got the right one, threw it wide open. 'Can't you hear that damned racket upstairs?'

Ruby looked up, startled. 'I'm sorry, I was asleep.'

'It's barely an hour since breakfast,' he sniffed the air with an expression of disgust. 'Are you drunk? While your business goes bust, your staff abandon you and one of your ghastly grand-children murders one of her sisters! Get up and sort your house out woman.'

Her eyes flashed a warning. 'Don't speak to me as though I were a skivvy. My business is my business, you go and tend to your own affairs.'

He laughed sarcastically. 'So, there's a spark of life left in you, praise be. Now, it's clear poor Juliet has given up, will you come up with me to check on the children?'

Ruby sighed and shook her head. 'Leave us alone, Juliet will calm the girls down, she always does.'

'But for how long? She has a new position to go to. I imagine she's sitting up there, counting the hours until she can leave.

'You're sitting here wallowing in self-pity, and things are falling apart. Mary's all things, cook, cleaner, nursemaid, and quite frankly I fear she'll be unable to cope with her multitude of thankless tasks for very much longer.'

Ruby frowned at him. 'Oh, Hugh, stop.'

He stifled a cry of frustration. 'Wake up and take care of your responsibilities, you have a family and a business to attend to.'

He might not have spoken. She reached out a shaking hand to pour a drink, her face impassive. He leapt across the room and snatched both glass and decanter from her, dashing them at the wall. The crash startled her and silenced the screaming children.

'Mary!' He shouted, knowing she had her ear pressed to the door.

'We've had an accident in here, a brush and a pot of coffee would be useful if that could be arranged.' He turned back to Ruby.

'Go and wash your face, you're a disgrace. We'll have coffee and talk about your business.'

She folded her arms and leaned back in her chair a mutinous expression on her face.

'You can be as stubborn as you choose, but I'm not leaving until I know you're back in control, so…' He removed his coat, sat down and picked up a book.

Ruby glared, but he sat quite comfortably flicking through the book until she left the room. Mary bent to clear the shattered glass.

'She's drinking too much.' Not a question but a statement.

'And eating nothing.' Mary agreed.

'Well, you've made it your work to spoil her, but I hope you'll break the habit of lifetime and back me up now. I can't ignore this, but I need to know you're with me.'

'I'm with you.'

They had a hasty conversation that sent Mary off in search of an empty packing case which she had moved into the little sewing room, a place Ruby barely knew existed.

She walked swiftly around the house removing every bottle and decanter she could find and placed them in the packing case which she covered with a velvet drape.

That done she made her way back to the kitchen where she made a pot of coffee, which she carried upstairs to Hugh and Ruby, who sat in silence.

Mary noted splashes on the front of Ruby's dress indicated she had at least rinsed her face, although she'd not bothered to glance in the mirror to sort out her ratty hair.

She lowered the tray onto a table and made to leave the room, not liking the ugly snarl on Ruby's face.

'No, Mary, you should stay.' Hugh said.

Ruby didn't speak so Mary sat down.

'Good. Now I want to hear your plans, firstly for your grandchildren, then Sansome Springs.' He pulled out his writing materials and put his head on one side ready to listen.

'What are you playing at Hugh? What do you care about my grandchildren or my business?'

'Ah, you're coming out of your drunken stupor, well done. Drink some coffee and answer my question.'

'For God's sake, can't you leave me alone?' Her voice wavered piteously.

'Sadly not. Those neglected girls are my family too and I know my duty. Your business is going to crash any day now, that means I'll be called upon to support you and them.'

Mary's eyes flicked anxiously back and forth.

'They're not being neglected, that's a dreadful accusation.' Ruby spoke quietly and without passion.

'They've been cared for by Juliet but she's leaving tomorrow. And you can't deny your business is a sinking ship because you have no idea what is going on, good or bad!'

Hugh poured himself a cup of coffee and bit into a great slice of cake, spilling crumbs all around.

Ruby watched him through narrowed eyes. 'I've had a difficult time, but Sansome Springs is in good hands and we'll get through. There's nothing for you to involve yourself in.' Her words lacked conviction.

He shook his head pityingly. 'But I am involved and there's no going back. Sansome Springs was mired in debt and, because you were unwilling to act, I settled all the outstanding accounts. You'll need to repay me, and I look forward to hearing when that will be done. Unless you want to give me shares, of course.'

Ruby leapt to her feet in frustration and walked to the dresser, she whirled around, a look of fury on her face. 'Where's my brandy?' She demanded as Mary lowered her gaze and Hugh smiled grimly.

'Business first.'

'I won't be told how to live. I've made my own way alone and...'

He sighed theatrically and raised his hand to his brow. 'Oh no, not that again. We all know you've suffered more than anyone else, and quite honestly, we're sick of hearing it. Grow up and appreciate what you have. You're sitting here in a drunken stew, feeling sorry for yourself. Where's your self-respect?'

Colour flooded Ruby's cheeks, then flowed out again. She dropped back into her chair and said very quietly, 'Don't shout at me, I'm sad and tired.'

Hugh nodded to Mary who went over and wrapped her arms around Ruby who allowed herself to be held as she cried like her heart was breaking.

Hugh went up to the top floor to rescue the despairing Juliet. 'Go and have a rest.' He told her. 'I'll stay for an hour or so.'

She left the room briskly, not needing to be told twice.

'Uncle Hugh! Uncle Hugh!'

He sat patiently as they took turns showing him the new tricks they had learned, vying for his attention and snapping at each other like puppies.

He was more used to the company of boys, one small girl he could manage, three was utterly terrifying!

Ruby wiped her eyes and sniffed deeply. 'Have I been very difficult?'

'Difficult?' Mary repeated in a wondering tone, putting her head to one side. 'If I'd had an education like yours I might find a better word to describe what you've been like, I'll allow *difficult* to suffice.'

'Well I'm sorry. Losing Bella was just too painful, on top of everything else. It was like a blanket was thrown over me and I couldn't see a way out, so I let the thing wrap itself around me, so that nothing else could hurt me.'

Mary said nothing. It was rare for them to talk about feelings, their lives together had been built on an understanding that went beyond words. But she couldn't bear for things to carry as they were and if Ruby needed to say this then she'd listen for as long as it took.

'I don't know how to carry on, how to be me. I've never been this afraid. Everything I've cared about has been broken or taken from me.'

Mary pulled back. 'Well, that's a slap in the face for me then, not to mention those girls.'

'Oh, don't pout, you know what I mean.'

'I'm a bit sick of hearing one thing but being expected to know it means another. It's time you woke up and considered the folks you live with.

'What happened didn't just happen to you. I lost my friend too. Your sister is widowed with a handful of kids. Poor little Eliza lost her parents and turned to you. There's a lot of heartbreak around here and we need to stop looking after *you* and start looking after each other. I can't go on like this. I've devoted my life to you, but I need something back, or are you ready to throw me away?'

Ruby dashed her tears away impatiently. 'No, oh no. Don't say that. You've been there from the start, I depend on you.'

Mary folded her arms and sucked her teeth. This was first. Ruby liked to call the tune and watch others dance along.

'I'm too old for this messing about. I always believed you loved me, as well as found me useful, but I'm doubting that now. I'm not your maid, and I won't act like one for another day. We're partners, or we'll go our separate ways!'

Shocked silence.

Mary looked for a sign that the girl she'd fallen in love with was still in there somewhere.

Ruby reflected on the time she'd been alone and terrified and Mary, a stranger, had been there to help her along.

'You gave me my first taste of hot chocolate.' She said.

'Aye, I stole it for you. What a risk I took, he'd have whipped me for sure. But you stood there, scared to death and as skinny as you like, but with your head held high. I so wanted to make you smile.'

'And you were laughing and as sweet and warm as his chocolate. Please forgive me Mary?'

'No more drinking?'

'I'll try.'

'You'll do more than try.'

They held each other, both appalled at how close they'd come to losing everything.

'We should go up, it's dreadfully quiet and I'm afraid those Morgan girls may have been too much for him.'

Her mouth was dry, and her head pounded, but she forced a smile. 'Well then, let's get to work.'

An affair of a very awful nature occurred in Worcester the week before last.

During the earlier part of the day on the Sunday, a woman living in St Martin's parish went several times to public houses for liquor, which she obtained. In the evening she went to one of these houses for more liquor and stayed there upwards of two hours. Several men were assembled in the house, some of whom gave her gin and ale.

At about nine o'clock she was led home from this house intoxicated, with part of her clothes off her back and cursing and blaspheming in a horrid manner.

She was put to bed and, it is shocking to add, was found dead early the next morning.

(Copyright and courtesy of the Worcester News)

CHAPTER FORTY-SEVEN

Ruby hadn't regained her happiness, or found peace, but she was no longer defeated and every day she moved closer to picking up the pieces of her life.

Her first battle had been to convince Juliet not to leave them, and it was hard fought. Juliet loved the girls, but she was tired, and she'd lost trust in Ruby, having seen her at her worst. She wasn't convinced that she was back in control.

She was persuaded to stay, but only agreed on the understanding that her hours would run from lunch until supper. She'd supervise both those meals, and the time in between, but mornings and evenings were to be her own.

Ruby accepted, knowing this was the best she was going to get. The girls felt safe with Juliet, so hanging on to her was crucial.

Ruby accepted that this was problem she'd caused because, despite her fine words, she'd handed her responsibility on to someone unqualified and had worn the girl out in the process. She'd have to do a better job.

When she felt the crippling waves of black misery approach, she took herself of for a walk and didn't come back until they'd gone. She stopped drinking entirely, and turned to the newspaper, or her accounts, for entertainment when the girls slept.

She kept herself busier than ever. Barnabus had been quite valiant in the face of her stubbornness, both in terms of the forbidden Spa opening - a roaring success - and then in approaching Hugh when he realised the finances were in disarray. But he couldn't be left to shoulder everything.

Once she'd thanked him and apologised for her neglect he surprised her with proposals he had to further develop the Spa. He'd grown in confidence and no longer needed her guidance. He spoke unhesitatingly about what must be done and what needed to change.

She had to bite her tongue, *she* was the spirit of the pleasure gardens. Yet she recognised his pride and ambition and was grateful he shared her passion.

It was that moment of clarity that led to their formal partnership. She decided that Sansome Springs ownership would be divided into four equal shares. One to be retained by herself, one by Mary, one by Barnabus and the fourth was for Richard.

She'd never considered taking partners, but Hugh had set her thinking when he'd paid her bills for her. She considered giving the girls a third each, but she couldn't leave Baranabus and Mary with nothing, and she had years left to decide what to do for the girls.

As a partner he'd earn a better wage and would be entitled to twenty five percent of the profits. He shook her hand so vigorously she winced.

'I'll never let you down, you changed my life.' He tripped over his words as he spoke of Dora, the young woman loved, now they could afford to marry.

His joy cracked through the shell of sadness she wore. She smiled as she accepted an invitation to join his wedding party before reminding him that he had yet to propose.

'But this time I'm sure of my lady.' He said with a rueful smile, remembering his unwelcome proposal to Ruby years before.

'Dora works hard and shares my dream of having enough money to afford a family house with a small garden. She takes care of her brother and sisters, so we need somewhere suitable for us all. That's all we've been waiting for.'

Mr Bell, drawing Master, having removed from Broad Street, Worcester to St Johns, Bedwardine, near this City (on the Bransford Road near the turnpike), takes this opportunity of respectfully acquainting his friends and patrons that specimens of his drawing in oil or water colour may be seen at his house or at Mr Hickey's, print seller, in Foregate Street, Worcester.

Mr Bell begs leave to inform those ladies and gentlemen or their families, who wish to be instructed in the elegant accomplishment of painting or drawing that they will receive many advantages while under his tuition.

(Copyright and courtesy of the Worcester News)

CHAPTER FORTY-EIGHT

The bell above Pargeters door announced her presence to everyone in the store. She'd neglected her sister shamefully and had to make amends but, being uncertain about her reception, she held her head high and refused to show it.

Her eyes scanned the shop, taking in the gleaming bottles on the shelves and rich glow of the mahogany counter.

A young man in a grey work coat approached her.

'Miss Morgan seeking a moment with Mrs Pargeter.' She said crisply.

Ellie was beside her seconds, smiling broadly and kissing her cheek before leading her through to a small room hidden behind a curtain. With no hesitation she wrapped her arms around her sister and Ruby was enveloped in the familiar cloud of lavender that was so much a part of her sister. It made her feel safe while at the same time highlighting her own shabby appearance.

'I've missed you, how are you?'

'I should be asking how you are. I've been so neglectful, but I couldn't seem to wake myself up. You've had to bear so much alone, I hate myself for my weakness.'

'I'm perfectly well. Come upstairs, let's have tea and compare notes on how well we've dealt with our losses.'

Ellie settled her sister in a comfortable chair by the window and kept up a stream of chatter as she made tea for them both.

'I'm content. I decided to keep all this going purely for the sake of the boys, but I have to say it's given me a new lease on life. I cope rather well in the world of business, and am developing a thirst for making changes, much to the dismay of the men who worked alongside Harold for so long.'

She shrugged, their opinion was nothing to her. 'The boys are happy enough, Harold wasn't a natural or affectionate father. They were shocked, and saddened, by his death, but our home is happier without him. Isn't that a wicked thing to admit?'

Ruby shook her head in denial, 'He was a miserable bully and you're all better off without him.'

Ellie held her tongue, longing to unburden herself, but realising her sister wasn't strong enough to lean on.

The last time they'd met was the week of Harold's death. Ruby had come to offer support, but it had been clear to Ellie that she was barely functioning and certainly not able to help in any way.

On seeing Ruby in the shop, Ellie hoped this visit was a sign that her sister was recovering but now, sitting close to her she had her doubts.

She was bone thin and desperately pale, her hair was lank, and her dress was not as clean as it could have been. She might be better than she was, but she still had a long way to go.

'How are you, Ruby?'

She gulped for breath and blinked rapidly. 'I didn't think I could go on without her and I feel so guilty now because I've even found myself laughing. How can I, when she's not here? Some days, I hear the girls giggling and I could scream at them, how can they be so carefree, how can they not care what has happened? Bella was one of the most important people in my life and I don't want to let her go.'

'I understand. It took me a long time to appreciate what you loved about her. I kept my distance, and she knew I thought I was better than her, but, when I needed help, she was by my side. I know she did it for the love of you, but I came to admire her greatly.

'She became my guardian angel when things were as black as they could be for me. In my darkest hour she could make me laugh, she was outrageous and fearless, and I can fully understand how much she must have helped you all those years ago. I grieve for her, as does Mary.

'You seem to think that by being happy you're letting her go, but you're not. You'll always have happy memories of her, and she'll never be truly gone.'

'I don't know how to *be* without her. There was hole in me where you had been, and Bella filled it.'

Ellies finger twitched, but Ruby hung on to her.

'No. She didn't replace you, never that. But she helped me leave the past where it was and look forward.'

'What would she say, if she saw you like this? She wouldn't want you wasting the life that you've been given. Squandering the love others feel for you. Don't turn your back on all that, I promise you won't lose any more of her. Your memories are there, whenever you want them, they always will be. And we can talk about her, you, Mary and me. We won't forget her, ever.'

'I know. And it is changing, I can't say it's easier, but I'm getting used to it and I can't tell you how disloyal that makes me feel. Bella is dead and I'm getting used to it.'

Ellie reached across and squeezed her hand. 'No. No more tears.'

Ruby wiped her had across her eyes. 'No more tears. Hugh came to visit and made me see sense. I'd been drinking and moping and if you could have seen the way he looked at me. He was so disappointed and that me ashamed. I know I can't allow the girls to experience the kind of cold childhood we had. Being responsible for them helps.'

She straightened her gown and smiled weakly. 'Let's change the subject, tell me about Harold, you said there's more to know?'

Ellie hesitated. This was her sister, her twin, the one who never turned her back, the only one she could confide in, but she was damaged, her scars still raw. Her confession would wait.

'The moment's passed. Let's plan a day to get the children together, I want my boys to know and love their cousins. We can plot who might marry whom in the future.'

'I'd rather deal with all our dark issues today, then we can move on. We can enjoy seeing our children learn to love one another when we've laid our ghosts. I need to know if you killed Harold.'

Mrs A Guise, chemist and druggist of 68 Broad Street, Worcester, begs leave to return her most grateful thanks to her numerous friends for the very liberal support they have rendered her since the decease of her late husband, and informs them that she has taken into partnership Mr JW Lea, who served his apprenticeship with her husband and has since conducted the business, which will be in future carried on under the firm of Guise, Lea and Co.
(Copyright and courtesy of the Worcester News)

CHAPTER FORTY-NINE

Ellie's mind flipped back to the terrible night she'd finally begun to understand her husband. She didn't want to weigh Ruby down but, as the problem was solved, what harm could it do.

She'd just received the news of Bella's death and had been devastated. She'd managed to hold on to her emotions until the boys were in bed, but once they were asleep, she lay down and cried for the girl who'd given her the strength and support to make a better life for herself. Had she shown her how grateful she was? Had she even apologised for referring to her as 'that woman' for twenty years.

Oh Bella. She slipped into a fitful sleep and was shocked into wakefulness by a tapping on her door. She hastily grabbed a wrap and saw the door handle move.

Her heart began pounding and the skin at the back of her neck prickled. Harold had left her alone since her return and she was afraid that he was about to assert himself once more.

'I need to talk to you Ellie, I don't mean you any harm.'

The door moved inwards, and she flung herself bodily against it. She would not submit to him again! She leaned against the door and thought again of Bella. *You've got a backbone, try using it.*

Harold gasped as the door slammed shut, causing him to jerk back and drop the candle he held.

He took a step backwards and spoke louder. 'I must speak to you, Ellie. I won't hurt you I swear it.'

'You'll disturb the boys. Go away.'

'I need to speak to you tonight, if it has to be through a door, then so be it.'

'You're not coming in here. Go down to the parlour and light some candles, I'll dress and join you shortly.' She put her ear against the door and waited to hear his steps descend.

The creak of the parlour door told her he was gone, and she could safely move from the door.

His voice had been quiet, without the bullish tone she'd become accustomed to and she decided to hear what he had to say. She dressed hastily, needing the illusion of protection.

She approached the parlour and saw he'd lit several candles and left the door wide open. He remained where he was, outlined by the open window, and thanked her for trusting him. She nodded.

'I have some things to tell you, and you may be shocked, but I'll be grateful if you allow me to finish before questioning me. We only have tonight.'

She took a seat at the far side of the room and watched him carefully, almost feeling Bella watching over her.

'I should never have married you and I hope you'll feel able to forgive me one day.

'Clara and I… It was different, she'd always been my friend you see. We shared everything as we grew up, we loved each other dearly and I trusted her utterly.

'I wasn't a proper husband to her, but she hadn't expected me to be. She married me out of kindness and all she asked in return was a child or two. My father was pressing me to marry, and she took pity.'

Ellie watched him carefully, he never spoke about himself and had not mentioned Clara for a very long time. He sounded a different man to the one she'd married. A terribly sad man.

'Clara deserved better, but the pressure made me frantic, and she made it all so easy, and then of course, my family was satisfied and my life improved.'

She was startled to see tears on his cheeks but couldn't bring herself to offer comfort.

'I was wrong to marry you. I took advantage and was never the man you thought I was. No matter how hard you tried, you could never be right for me. I took my frustration out on you. It was not your fault that I imagined I could be content with a replacement Clara. She helped and advised me, and on occasions covered up for me, something you couldn't do. You don't know me, and I misled you.

'I've been reckless and am about to be exposed. I have unnatural needs that I battle with daily. Sometimes I lose the battle! On those occasions, I travel as far away as I'm able. I've never done anything to cause any talk about me in Worcester I swear it.

'Recently I met someone, and then I met him again. He was not important, but the freedom of being with someone who understood me was heady and I, well, I couldn't stay away.' He groaned. 'I didn't want to stay away.'

He stared into the flickering candle and she waited for him to continue. He drew in a deep breath and smiled sadly.

'I thought I saw him following me a few days ago but I wasn't certain. But, as I walked into the shop yesterday, I saw him leave. He's been in here and who knows who he's spoken to? It will all come out, and I can't prevent it.'

She saw genuine terror on his face and softened, knowing a tormented soul when she saw one. 'Perhaps the man you saw simply looked like the one you know.'

He shook his head emphatically.

'Maybe it was him and he wanted to see you again.' She offered.

'We're not talking about love Ellie.' He said bitterly. 'Don't put a romantic twist on this for God's sake. If he *has* found me it's for one reason only, he wants me to buy his silence.'

He told her he couldn't bear for the boys to know the truth about him. 'If I'm not around there will be no reason for him to saying or do anything.'

He handed her a bundle of papers which he said would clear up any questions relating to the business and the house, and then he showed her where he'd hidden some money.

'But if you're going away, surely you'll need this?' She asked as he shook his head.

'I treated you badly and I deserve to rot in hell for it. But I'm happy to know you'll be here to guide my sons through their lives.'

The silence in the room was absolute as the sisters looked at each other.

'I thought he was going to pack up and go, but he killed himself the following night.'

'I thought you'd killed him.' Ruby said.

Ellie shook her head.

'He was just a sad man, trying to hide what he really was and keep his reputation intact. I'll do all I can to see that in death he can be at peace. No-one must ever know what I've told you.

'It was a blessing to feel able to talk about it, but only with Ruby.'

'I won't tell a soul, but I think you've painted him more decent than he was. He was a swine to you.'

Ellie nodded her agreement. 'He was, but he's dead now and I don't want his boys to be upset by things that no longer matter. He's left us well provided for and dwelling on the past is not for me.'

Ruby frowned. 'Do you think that's what I've been doing?

'You've had worse than me to put up with. Losing someone you love dearly is much harder than losing someone who made your life a misery. But perhaps it's time to put your life back together. It'll be different, but it can be good if you'll give it a chance.'

'But...'

'No, let me finish. You're a business woman, first and foremost, and I think you need to get back to that. Do what you must to provide for the girls but stop trying to be something you're not. You can be a loving presence in their lives, without trying to be a mother to them.

'Really, you need to get your teeth into a project and let someone else do the mothering because it doesn't suit you. Half your trouble is you're bored and unsatisfied. Get to work and leave the nest building to those who know how to do it.'

Mr Dods, surgeon of High Street, Worcester, wants
immediately an active, steady stable boy.
(Copyright and courtesy of the Worcester News)

CHAPTER FIFTY

John Smith, clerk, porter, tea maker, sweeper up, and holder of secrets, peered through the window and cursed colourfully. Ruby was there, patrolling back and forth on the abandoned site behind the office, and getting in the way of his love life.

His breaktime habit was to scramble through this window and pop along to The Albion where he could enjoy a tankard of decent ale and - if Brew Butler was the worse for drink - a cuddle with his generous daughter. Everyone was happy.

He left the stock room and went back into the main office. 'She's out there again, wandering about and talking to herself. I reckon she's lost her bloody wits.'

Ann swallowed her irritation and spoke automatically. 'Don't be disrespectful.' She pulled on her coat and stepped outside, needing to know what was afoot.

She left the shelter of the courtyard and walked across the ground that had been destined for better things, until the bodies were found.

Coming out here must be a painful reminder for Ruby and she had to make sure she was not dwelling on the past.

'I thought I'd come out and see how you're keeping.'

The familiar smile flashed her way and eased her mind. Ruby was back in control that much was plain to see. 'I'm not here to get in your way, I don't plan to stay more than a few moments more. I just wanted to see what we left behind. This land must be put to some use.'

'Are you going to build...?'

Ruby put her hands up in denial. 'Not me. I've no stomach for it, but someone else has expressed an interest and I'm thinking things through.'

Ann kept a tactful silence as Ruby continued almost talking to herself. 'Something should be done, and the time feels right.'

She nodded her head in satisfaction and looked at Ann. 'What's causing all the running around that I see going on here?'

They walked towards the office. 'Another Royal visit, The Prince of Wales and the Duke of Sussex are intending to visit soon and I'm trying to get details about that, in addition to our usual load. There's to be a parade with bands and a lunch at the Guild Hall and everyone's flustered because it's unexpected.'

'We've only just seen the back of Gloucester, I wonder why they're all descending on us this year?'

A male voice chimed in. 'Maybe they've heard about what goes on at Sansome Springs, those brothers like a bit of fun, rumour has it.'

Ruby smiled at the man. 'It's good to see you, Jacob.'

'You too Ruby, though you're looking too thin if you ask me.'

His confidence had come on in leaps and bounds and he was less respectful than Ann thought proper.

She tutted in frustration. 'Jacob, really!'

He grinned cheekily, showing no remorse. 'Sorry ladies.' He sketched a bow and strode away.

'He's polite to everyone else.'

Ruby laughed. 'I wouldn't have him any other way. Is he doing well?'

'I never have to worry about a thing when he's around. He knows what needs to be done and can turn his hand to whatever's required. He's second to none at getting out and about and uncovering what's going on. People trust him.'

Ruby nodded made small talk for a few moments. She'd had to bolster herself to come back here, but she was glad she'd done it.

There was a better use for all this land and she was ready to forge ahead and make good.

A main of cocks is to be fought at Alex Monnox's Mitre Oak Inn, Hartlebury, between the gentlemen of Worcestershire and the gentlemen of Staffordshire on Monday, Tuesday and Wednesday next for five guineas per battle and £100 for the main.
(Copyright and courtesy of the Worcester News)

CHAPTER FIFTY-ONE

Since Hugh had assumed responsibility for shaking Ruby out of her lethargy they'd developed a greater respect for one-another.

She appreciated him doing what no-one else dared, and then standing beside her as she took tentative steps back into her world. He'd listen to her doubts and offer words of encouragement, urging her keep going, and celebrating her every success.

They met for dinner regularly, usually just the two of them. They'd talk about business concerns, or the demands of bringing up a family. Sometimes they'd reminisce.

Hugh sensed Ruby had something on her mind and patiently filled the time with idle chatter as he waited for her to speak, she kept little from him and he had time to wait for her to find the words.

She'd decided to share a dream with him. Something she'd never have imagined wanting before her life, and her priorities, had altered. She had money and influence, but neither had helped when she lost what she loved most.

She now felt a burning to desire to do something of lasting good, something to help others make the most of their lives.

It seemed so obvious once she'd thought of it but gaining Hugh's support was crucial. If she was on the right track, he'd be behind her all the way, but he was a clever man who questioned everything and if there was a flaw in her plan he'd spot it.

'Something on your mind Ruby? I'm perfectly happy, but we've now completed two circuits of Mary's kitchen garden, and I should send a message if I'm not to be home before dawn.'

'There is something I want to talk about.'

'Wouldn't you feel better once it's out in the open?'

A nod and a gulp of breath and she was off. 'I want you to help me open a school. A proper school with good tutors and the best facilities.'

He laughed out loud. 'Sam did an outstanding job, but even he couldn't make us fit to be educators.'

She thumped his arm playfully. 'Fool. I mean to build and fund a school! With a board of governors, a treasurer and a matron, everything as it should be. But we should select the right people to provide what we need, people who are qualified and agree that education must be available to all.

'We have a lot of children between us, all of whom must be educated. The thought of your boys going off and leaving Alice at home saddens me. I know what that feels like.'

Hugh stopped walking and turned to face her, eyebrows raised. 'You want me to build a school for *our* children and you're using *my* daughter's situation to pressure me?'

Ruby eyes sparkled. 'Yes, certainly I'm using it. She'd benefit, you can see that?'

'My dear girl, you must be mad.'

'Think about it though. If we got this right, we could keep our children close by and offer an education to so many others. I'll use all my power and influence to get the help we need. We could really make a difference.'

He sat down on the bench and looked up at her and she saw with a pang how much older and sadder he was these days. 'Hugh, you have so much to deal with and perhaps I shouldn't have brought this up, but I truly think a school that could take all of your children would help you so very much.'

He sighed deeply, and she held her breath. He hadn't laughed at her, and he hadn't yet given a flat no.

'The trouble with you, is you never perceive the obstacles in front of you and that can be exhausting for those around you. I know you're a good woman, but you have a shocking reputation. There's a gaming hell in your pleasure gardens for heaven sake. Do you honestly think that *anyone* will consider you a person fit to run a school?'

'Not a soul.' She grinned at the thought. 'I can't think of anything more damaging for me or the children. No, that's why I need you. I'll fund it, but I want no further involvement. The public face should be you. There's no stain on your reputation.'

'It's a ridiculous idea.' He spoke firmly, but she'd spotted the glimmer of interest that had fleetingly lit his face.

'Ha! You're tempted, aren't you? Come on, you're not one to back away from a challenge.'

'I'm not tempted in the least. I don't have the time required. I've got six children and a business to oversee. I'm not adding to my responsibilities.'

She persisted. 'I'll do all the preparation work and I have most of the money required. I own the land

and I'm prepared to do anything I can. We'll have school fees, and for every paying child, I want to offer a free place to a child born into circumstances like mine.

'We can do it. All we need is the veneer of respectability that you, and your name, has. It need not interfere in your life in any way.'

'Of course, it would interfere! A school is a serious undertaking, and I'd insist on being fully involved. Everything would have to be done properly.'

He shook his head impatiently. 'I'd foolishly imagined that having a houseful of children might have filled your days and yet you're as determined and dangerous as ever it would appear.'

Then he laughed in mock outrage. 'And may I add, my respectability is more than a veneer, it runs to my core, cheeky madam.'

Her face was alight with enthusiasm now, he was looking for reasons to go along with her and victory was hers.

'I see a void and I aim to fill it. Rich boys get a good education, rich girls get a poor education and poor children get nothing. We can be the ones to change that!'

'Your voice speaks Sam Thatcher's words.'

'Because he was right! I spoke to Betty Taylor this morning. Her sister's little one was caught trying to steal a pair of shoes. Old ones, from a pedlar. She's nine years old and has never had a shoe on her foot. I know she shouldn't steal, she knew she shouldn't steal, but the fact remains that a little girl just a few months older than your Alice is going to be flogged in public for taking something she was told to take.'

'I have no idea who Betty Taylor is or how her child is relevant to this issue?' He'd decided to make her work a bit harder for what she wanted.

'That child can't be saved, she'll be flogged in front of the church for stealing, and she'll be flogged at home for getting caught. She'll go hungry and be badly treated for the rest of her life and there's nothing anyone can do to save her.

'But we *can* do something to help other children born into poverty. An education, a purpose, a place to go to learn how to better themselves.

'I'm not saying if there had been a free school Betty's sister would have sent the child because I know that she wouldn't, that child was a workhorse since the day she was born, but the children we educate will grow into better parents, they'll learn, and that learning will spread. I want *you* to help *me* make it happen.

'A child born in St Andrews this morning has no future. If we do this then there would be a slim chance for them, and that's better than no chance at all.'

'Ah. You want me to educate other people's children and mine will get their own education, alongside the rabble?'

'You don't think that way Hugh so don't try it with me. You employ good men who would want their children educated if the means were available. You've never been one to think being poorer is being less important.'

'No, and I shouldn't have called them rabble, but I have high hopes for my children and I want to give them every opportunity to mix with the right sort of people.'

'As do most parents.' She retorted. He acknowledged the truth of that with a nod.

'I want you to help me, but I intend to gather support from a great many sources across the city to help children like me and Ellie.

'It was a lucky accident that gave us the education we had. You'd always have had one because your people could pay. Ours couldn't, or wouldn't, that was wrong then and it's wrong now, and if I don't do something about it then I'll have wasted every chance that came my way and I can't do that. I've been blessed, and I aim to share my blessings. Will you help me?'

'Why now?'

'I'm angry at the attitudes I've had to face trying to pay for an education for the girls. Twenty years ago, when I had little money and less confidence it was easier to source an education for Richard than it is today for them. I don't want a genteel governess to teach them how to sew and I will not send them to some ghastly place where they'll be taught to dance and play the piano. I want a school to give them a thorough grounding and there's no such thing for girls.'

'So why not open a school for girls?'

'Because it would be considered second best and I won't settle for that. I want a school good enough for the sons of men like you, that way I know the girls will get a fair deal.'

Hugh's face was a picture. The image of a child being flogged for stealing something was now firmly in his mind, the barbarity made him shudder.

Ruby had convinced him there should be a better way. He groaned and rubbed his hands over his eyes as she laughed jubilantly, knowing her first battle was won.

'People won't like it.' He warned.

'That's why I need your support. It will be the hardest thing we've attempted but it will also be the best thing.'

J Richards Commercial and Classical Academy in The Tything near Foregate Street, Worcester has re-opened. Young Gentlemen are liberally boarded, tenderly treated and diligently taught Writing, English Grammar and Composition, the Classics, Arithmetic, Geography and the use of Globes and Maps. The fee terms may be known by applying at the Academy.
(Copyright and courtesy of the Worcester News)

CHAPTER FIFTY-TWO

The standing joke of Worcester's insecure gaol was catapulted to a crisis when Lord Chief Baron Macdonald arrived at the Guild Hall to hold the quarter sessions, only to discover that *all* the prisoners he was to try had escaped.

He was incandescent with rage and ordered the council to have the situation remedied before his next visit or they'd lose their jobs.

He spoke to the newspaper and was highly critical of the way Worcester was managed. His angry words carried great weight and attracted sneering reports from across the country.

There was no choice, taxes must be raised, and a new gaol built. There were protests and meetings, for and against, but the matter could no longer be swept out of sight.

A secure gaol at the other side of the city would be built, it would be a wise investment for the security, and self-respect, of Worcester.

Two artichoke fields along Salt Lane were purchased and work began on the £18000.00 project.

The furore and debate lasted for six months and kept much of the citizens too busy to worry about the work going on in Sidbury. The extensive building out past the cathedral was almost completed before anyone noticed.

A small crowd gathered to watch and gossip as the stone, carved with the initials HH, was lowered into place at the top of the arch over the massive wooden doors.

Once Hugh had agreed that a school was a good idea there was no stopping him. He missed no opportunity to talk about it and had, over the past year, earned a measure of support, generally from those less able to pay for schooling.

Any potential investor or interested parent was invited along to see the work in progress, much to the irritation of Francis, who as head of the project, was constantly having to stop and listen as Hugh talked about what he was offering to the children of Worcester.

Suspicion lingered. Why would a wealthy man want children of the poor to be educated alongside his own? Dubious eyes were trained on this venture and he knew any failure would be seized upon with relish.

Despite inviting every acquaintance to come and look over the school no-one had yet proved willing to pay to have their own child educated here.

When he'd mentioned an open day, Ruby assured him that every busy-body in Worcester would turn up, whether they had children or not.

They came in their droves, but still no-one took advantage.

Hugh had spent the greater part of his time selecting the best tutors, their educational abilities had to be strong, but he needed more than that. He delved into the backgrounds of every single one, talking to their friends and then to the friends of their friends, seeking men who agreed with his vision. Men who agreed that being born to poor parents was no reason to remain poor. Men who felt that a good education must be available to everyone. He had to weed out those who said one thing but believed another.

The school had tutors and a matron, it was time to work on building up a reputation.

The school opened with sixteen pupils. Half a dozen Daventors, three Pargeters, three Morgans, and four orphans from St Andrews.

The Morgan girls loved being at school, flourishing as part of the dozen cousins, as their male cousins dubbed them. Alice quickly became best friend to Eliza.

Freddy Daventor ordered his brothers to shun the Pargeter boys. Stating they were the sons of a shopkeeper and not true family. Freddie revelled in his status as the daring and outrageous one and constantly sought new ways for the others to prove their worth.

The Pargeters cared not a jot for Freddie or his attempts to lord it over them. He wasn't the most senior, that was clever Arthur who smiled absently at everyone he met. He'd effectively take Freddie to task when he uttered something truly offensive.

The quartet from St Andrews were initially wide-eyed and uncertain, but their true natures quickly surfaced. They'd been brought up hard and were not about to take any bullying lying down. They'd fight the nobs for the respect they wanted.

Ruby stayed close enough to see, but not be seen. Converting what had been Richard's house, into a lending library. He'd never return, and this was a project she could make her own.

The dilapidated area, once nothing more than a stop for travellers who arrived after the city after the gates were barred for the night, was transformed into a thriving and attractive part of the city.

A fine school, a newspaper, a lending library, all in the shadow of the cathedral.

Six months after the school opened, a bookbinder set up a shop, quickly followed by an artist offering classes in drawing and the use of watercolours.

Ruby never visited the school or met any of the people involved in it. She knew she'd built something important and that was enough.

The magistrates of Worcestershire held a meeting in this City on Thursday to take into further consideration the site of the proposed new county prison at Worcester. After discussion it was agreed that it should be erected on a new site. A piece of land opposite the north end of the infirmary has been fixed upon by the magistrates as the place of erection.

(Copyright and courtesy of the Worcester News)

If you enjoyed this story you may also want to explore these titles from the same author:

The Harlot's Garden
The Harlot's Pride
The Harlot's Horde
Losing Hope
An Ordinary Girl

Printed in Poland
by Amazon Fulfillment
Poland Sp. z o.o., Wrocław